Confessions
of a Bitter
Secret Santa

candy apple books . . .
just for you.
sweet. fresh. fun.
take a bite!

CONFESSIONS OF A BITTER SECRET SANTA

by Lara Bergen

SCHOLASTIC INC.

New York Toronto London Auckland Sydney
Mexico City New Delhi Hong Kong Buenos Aires

ISBN-13: 978-0-545-04668-8
ISBN-10: 0-545-04668-8

12 11 10 9 8 7 6 5 4 3   8 9 10 11 12 13/0

Printed in the U.S.A.
First printing, October 2008

TO SECRET SANTAS EVERYWHERE

✳ CHAPTER ONE ✳

First off, let me set the record straight: I love Christmas and the holidays and all that stuff as much as the next girl. I mean, with a name like Noel, how could I possibly not?

Some people even ask me if I was *born* on Christmas, with a name like Noel. But I have to tell them, No; I was born on August 15 — the same day as my great-grandfather Noel . . . (rhymes with Cole). Apparently, my parents had been so sure I'd be a boy, they'd promised to name me after him no matter what. Classic, right? Oh, well . . . I'm just glad they were nice enough to pronounce *my* name like a girl's.

But back to Christmas . . . here's the thing: No matter how great the holidays usually are, I am positively certain that even Mrs. Claus herself would have had a hard time *ho-ho-ho*-ing this year. I mean, think about it. What if each and every one of your friends was going somewhere totally awesome for winter break, and feeling positively *compelled* to talk about it constantly, while all you had to look forward to was a week and a half cooped up in your house with your parents, your little sister, and — as if that weren't bad enough — another one on the way!

Okay, don't get me wrong. I love babies as much as the next girl — of *course*. I just prefer it when they're other people's babies . . . not my own mother's. I mean, come on. She's, like, practically forty-*five*. Yeah, I know. I *know*. You'd think a person who wanted three kids would have had them all together — like everyone else's mother. *What was she thinking?* you might ask. Seriously. Who knows?!

But that was all just the tip of the iceberg, as they say. It got *much* worse, let me tell you. Seriously.

It all started in homeroom — seventh-grade English, to be precise — on the Friday before the last week before winter vacation.

I was sitting at my desk, pretty much minding my own business, trying to answer the list of questions written on the board, and trying *not* to hear the conversations going on all around me.

It wasn't easy, though.

Like, I'm pretty sure Isabelle was talking about what an awesome time she was going to have skiing in Colorado:

"West Coast skiing is *so* much better than East Coast. It's a proven fact. I *know*."

While Colin was informing her of how bogus her theories were:

"I guess you haven't been to Vermont," he scoffed. "We go there *every* winter and it is *sweet*. And why do you waste your time skiing, anyway? Riding's *way* more fun."

"Yeah," his friend Mason chimed in. "Skiing's for losers."

"Snowboarding rules!"

"It really *is* more fun," agreed Abby.

"Whatever," said Isabelle dismissively.

Meanwhile, I think I can say for sure that Tallulah and Ruby were describing in excruciating detail the house their families would be sharing (talk about *unfair*) on some exclusive Florida Key somewhere.

"It's right on the beach," Tallulah explained. "But it's also got a pool."

"And a hot tub!" Ruby added. "Don't forget that!"

"Hey, I'm going to be staying on the beach in Cancún!" Olivia informed them. "We can totally wave to each other across the Gulf of Mexico!"

"Cool!"

"Awesome!"

Enough already! I thought.

"Aw, you guys are so lucky," Melanie sighed. "I wish I could just sit and hang out on the beach and wave to people."

I couldn't help it. I turned to her, suddenly hopeful. Was Melanie staying home, too, I wondered? Would there be *someone* to hang out with over vacation after all?

"Seriously," she went on, "after all the hikes and everything my parents have planned for us in Costa Rica, I think I'm going to need another vacation when we get home!"

There is a very good chance I groaned.

I'm pretty sure the only person not going on and on and *on* about their winter vacation — except me, of course — was my BFF, Claire. But that's not because she wasn't going somewhere awesome after school let out, as well. (If you can

4

stand it, think Hawaii.) No, it's because she knew how bummed out the whole subject made me. (She's not my best friend for no reason, after all.) And yes, I think I had made it pretty clear over the course of that week that if I had to hear about luaus and leis and helicopter rides over volcanoes on top of everything else, I might not be responsible for my actions. . . .

And yet, you may ask, weren't we sitting there in English class? How in the world could all those inane conversations be going on?

Well, the answer's pretty simple: substitute. And not just any substitute either. Miss "Just-Call-Me-Summer" Lee, who, between her iPod headphones and her texting, probably wouldn't have known if the class had stood up and put on a Broadway show.

Not that I'm complaining; that's the perfect sub, if you ask me. It's just on that particular day I could have used a little more *intervention*. I mean, is one "Please stop talking and do your work" too much to ask, really? But no. After a "Hey, guys! How ya doin'?" and a "Looks like your teacher had something better to do today. Ha-ha!," the sub (who looked, by the way, even younger than Claire's sister, Layla, who's in high school; or maybe even Claire herself, who everyone thinks looks at least fifteen) quickly wrote out the questions Mrs. Bailey had left for us, sat down, turned up her volume, took out her phone, and left me there to endure fifty minutes of pure torture.

Or maybe make that forty.

Because to everyone's surprise, at exactly 9:10, Summer suddenly stood up, pulled off her headphones, and made an announcement.

"Oh, man! I almost forgot! Mrs. Bailey left one more thing for you all to do."

Right away, vacation chatter gave way to worried rumbles.

The sub held up a piece of paper. "Don't sweat. It looks like fun . . . let's see . . . yeah. She wants you guys to do Secret Santa next week 'in lieu,' she says, 'of a midterm exam'!" Her mouth opened in a wide smile that showed off the silver stud in the middle of her tongue. "I know!" she said. "How cool!"

Secret Santa! "Cool" was right. Claire spun around, excited, and I gave her a high five. Way to go, Mrs. Bailey!

Around us, the classroom hummed with all sorts of "Really?"s and "No way!"s, as everyone wondered what our teacher could be thinking. I mean, who would have thought a teacher — even one as totally awesome as Mrs. Bailey — would actually go and do something so totally awesome?

"Hey, don't ask me," Summer said, shrugging. "All I know is she wants everyone in homeroom to write down their name, locker number, and combination on a piece of paper and pass it up to me. Then I get to hand a name back to each of you, and that's whose Secret Santa you get to be."

She crossed her arms with satisfaction . . . and snuck a quick glance at her phone.

We all looked at one another until finally, Isabelle spoke up.

"And then what?"

"Oh, right." The sub looked up. "Good question." Her eyebrows slid together — the ring in her left one rising up. "Let's see . . ." She studied her paper. "Okay . . . right. It looks like you're supposed to spend the weekend and next week thinking about the person you get and what you can surprise them with that will be *meaningful* and *special*. She says you should plan on leaving something small in their locker every day next week, through Friday. And feel free to decorate, too, if you li—"

"Oh! Oh! Miss . . . uh . . . Summer!"

Melanie's arm swung like a windshield wiper across the back of the room.

"Yeah?" Summer pointed to her.

"What happens if you're not going to be here next Friday?" Melanie asked. "I mean, what if you're going to Costa Rica that day? Should your Secret Santa leave your Friday gift for you on Thursday?"

While my eyes rolled, the sub actually stopped and looked as if she were really trying to think.

"Got me," she finally said. "Guess you gotta ask Mrs. Bailey on Monday. Costa Rica, huh? Nice!"

An eager chatter began to scamper across the room, but Summer was quick to raise her hands to tame it. "Hang on a sec, guys. There's just a couple more rules here. Listen up: 'One: Under no circumstances should you share locker combinations. Two: There will be no trading names. Three: There will be no *sharing* names. Four: Every student in the class must participate.' And 'Five: You are not to spend more than ten dollars, total. Remember,' she says, 'the object of Secret Santa is to try to get to know your classmates better and show them that you care for them, not to impress them or anyone else.' Oh, and 'Have fun!' Man . . ." The sub nodded. ". . . that's really . . . nice."

Nice? I thought to myself. This wasn't *nice* . . . it was perfect! After all, this was exactly what I'd been waiting for all year: the chance to get to know one of my classmates better and to show him that I cared for him . . . a lot!

Instantly, my eyes shot over to the dark-haired, kind of quiet, *very* cute classmate in question . . . desk closest to the dictionary, fourth row from the front.

Nick Holiday, to be precise.

He was slumped back in his chair (in that cute way he always is), picking some loose rubber off the side of his Adidas.

I gulped and felt my mouth go dry (in that way *it always* does) and quickly closed my eyes.

Please, I pleaded silently, *please, please,* please. *Please let me be Nick Holiday's Secret Santa. Please!*

I knew with absolute certainty that if I could just have this one wish granted, I'd never have to wish for anything else again. Ever. I mean, I wouldn't need to. I wouldn't care anymore that I kept getting C's on my French quizzes. I wouldn't care that I hadn't gotten a lead role in the fall musical. I wouldn't care that my precious winter vacation was being wasted staying at home waiting for my mom to have a baby. I wouldn't even care that my mom was *having* a baby. Because I knew, no doubt about it, that if I could just be

Nick's Secret Santa, I could finally stop crushing on him and get him to actually like me back!

I mean, it was simple. We'd been friends — *just* friends — since he moved here in fourth grade, and I knew everything he liked. His favorite band (easy: Green Day); his favorite team (Colts, all the way); his favorite color (light blue, *not* navy); his favorite ice cream (chocolate chip cookie dough — mine too!). You name it: He liked it, I had it noted (no kidding, really) and (at least mentally) neatly filed away.

You'd think he'd have noticed by now, but he had absolutely no idea.

But if I could actually get a whole week to surprise him with all those things he really, really liked . . . well, then he'd *have* to like me, wouldn't he? He'd *have* to think, *Wow! Here's a girl who really knows me . . . who understands me . . . who gets me, at last. Who cares if she has braces and frizzy hair that simply refuses to grow? Who cares if her mom isn't actually getting fat — like she'd said in the fall — but is actually having a baby? We were meant to be together. Forever. Period.*

"Come on, guys. Class is almost over. I need your names and locker info, pronto!" Summer called.

I quickly scribbled:

on a piece of paper. Then I folded it in half and turned to look at Nick again. This time, though, he caught me (in that way he sometimes does). I tried not to wince as I hurried to find something else to stare at . . . the clock? The door? Billy Butcher's bizarre haircut? (Think mohawk meets mullet. Seriously. Where did *that* come from?) But at the same time I *had* to see what Nick's paper looked like when he passed it up to Summer. After all, in order to *be* Nick's Secret Santa, I had to get his name somehow.

I held my hand up to my face and peeked through the gap between my first and middle fingers (most discreetly, I assure you). Nick had turned back to his paper and, after writing what he had to, casually folded it once, then twice, into adorably crooked fourths. He handed it to Billy, who was in front of him, who handed it up ahead . . . then went back to work intently on the ragged sole of his shoe.

I passed my own paper up to Claire, but it was Nick's paper I followed, from hand to hand to Summer, and into a stack with all the others.

11

"Thanks, guys," said Summer as she breezily leafed through them. "Let's see . . . five, ten, fifteen . . . hang on . . . aren't there twenty of you? I only have nineteen." She quickly counted them again. "Who's still got theirs? Hmm?"

She looked around the room, and the rest of the class did, too — all but me, that is. (My eyes were otherwise occupied, as I think I already explained.)

"Well, did we drop one?" said the sub when nobody responded. "Anybody see one? Anywhere?"

"Nope."

"Not me."

"Uh . . . no."

"Oh, brother," Summer sighed. She set the pile down on the desk and put her hands on her hips. "Come on, guys. You heard the rules. Everyone has to do this. Who hasn't yet? Come on."

For the first time all period, the room was completely silent.

After a second the sub's gaze came to rest somewhere behind me, and one by one, everyone else's eyes drifted there, too. I, of course, was determined to keep my eyes on Nick's paper, but I guess I finally decided it wasn't going anywhere, and after a second I turned around, too. It was easy then to see what the class's problem was: the tight-lipped, red-cheeked new girl, Mia Malone.

Now, don't get me wrong. I'm as friendly as the next girl. (Okay, maybe a little less sometimes . . . but sometimes a whole lot more.) And I'm definitely not the type to talk about you behind your back. (That is *so* not cool!) But I have to say right now that it was pretty common knowledge among all my friends and me that Mia was about the most stuck-up girl in our whole school. *Why?* you ask. Well, I'll tell you.

For one thing, she'd moved here from New York back in the middle of October and had *still* barely spoken to any of us. I mean, not even a simple "Good morning" or "Want to come over and swim in my pool?" (Okay, maybe it was too cold. But still.) And, well, it was pretty obvious to us exactly what she was thinking: *These kids are* so *not as cool as the ones at my old school.* I mean, we all knew her dad was some important business-guy-something, and we all knew that she lived in one of the biggest houses in town, and if she didn't think we were good enough to talk to, well then, what could you do?

But not wanting to do Secret Santa? Well, that was just rude!

"I'm sorry," said Summer, walking slowly back toward Mia. "I don't mean to single you out, but are we still waiting for *you*?"

Mia's head tilted down and her hair formed a sort of shiny gold force field around her.

"Yes . . . do I have to?" came a cold, stiff voice from beneath the thick, blond veil.

"She speaks!" murmured Ruby with a chuckle.

The sub shrugged. "Well, yeah, you do."

I couldn't hear her sigh, but I could see Mia's shoulders rise, then fall dramatically, and I remember thinking how crazy she was to make such a big deal of the whole thing. Clearly, she thought Mrs. Bailey's Secret Santa idea was a waste of her precious time, and honestly I wished the sub would go ahead and let her out of it. I mean, I had to pity whoever's Secret Santa Mia turned out to be — and the poor person who had to be hers even more. *Imagine,* I thought, *the thankless job of getting to know her!*

Besides, it was already 9:20 and the bell was about to ring and if she didn't write down her name soon, we were all going to be late to second period. . . .

I just wanted to get Nick Holiday's name already and go!

Of course, I turned to look at Claire, who was just as bewildered as me. We shared a

14

"what-is-with-her" eye roll, then shook our heads with relief as she finally scribbled down her name and locker info.

"Thanks," said the sub, almost exactly as the bell rang. She cringed a little and let it finish, then added Mia's paper to the rest of the stack and hurried to the door.

"Okay, cool!" she said, clearly relieved that this crisis was over and probably eager to text the drama to some friend via her phone. "Why don't you guys just line up and grab a name as you go. Oh! And take a sec to make sure you don't get your own! Ha!" She tossed back her head and let out a laugh as she leaned against the door. "That would be just great, wouldn't it?!"

Yes! I thought, *This is perfect!* as I stood up and grabbed my books. All I had to do was get myself into the right place in the line. And so, as the class assembled into something I suppose you could *loosely* call a line, I tried to figure out exactly where Nick's name was in Summer's pile.

No problem, of course. Though I'd taken my eyes off his paper for a minute, I could still tell it easily by its odd, mismatched corners. It was in the middle, I was positively sure.

"Hey, no cuts!" said Colin as I angled for position.

"Oh, relax, Colin," said Claire. She was even closer to Summer than he was and loyally reached out to stake a claim for me beside her. "We've still got to get all the way to French. Let us go."

"Oh, it's okay," I said, gallantly waving Colin on. "After you, sir," I said, smiling. "Oh, and you too, Mason. Please, go on."

Claire looked at me with that look she sometimes gets when she thinks I'm acting crazy.

"What are you waiting for?" she asked me. "Don't you want to find out whose Secret Santa you are?"

"Not yet," I whispered. "Hang on." I let Courtney go after Mason, and then Abby after her . . . then — *gulp!* — Nick himself, along with Billy and Isabelle. Then at last I tugged on Claire's hand. "Okay!" I said. "Let's go!"

Dragging Claire behind me, I stepped up in front of Summer, then looked down and suddenly stopped. *Hang on,* I thought. I could have sworn I was getting Nick's paper. But the one beneath it looked just the same!

"Go ahead," said Summer. "It's just paper. It won't bite."

I know it won't bite, I thought. But which one did I *want*? My whole future lay in which name I chose, after all. I couldn't mess this up!

16

Meanwhile, the natives still behind me were getting restless.

"Come on, Noel."

"Move it, Moore!"

"Hurry up!"

I'll be honest; I was paralyzed. But then the fog began to clear. *Trust your instincts,* my mom always told me. So that's exactly what I did. I swung Claire around in front of me and let *her* take the phony name . . . while I swooped in and took the genuine thing.

I sighed as I walked out after Claire into the hall. *Phew,* I thought. *That was a close one!* In my eagerness, I'd almost made a *terrible* mistake. But everything was going to be perfect now, I knew.

I hugged the paper to my chest for a moment. Then I held my breath as, at last, I slowly opened it up.

*C*HAPTER *T*WO

Yep. You guessed it. You're totally right. The paper that I got was not Nick Holiday's at all.

I could have cried. (In fact, I might have.)

And yes, in most disaster epics, that would have been bad enough. But not in mine. Oh no! My story gets even worse!

Because when I unfolded the miserable paper, *this* is what it said:

Mia Malone

1142

19–33–8

"What?" asked Claire. "What's the matter?"

I guess I must have been moaning.

"Oh, just look!" I said, holding the sheet out with disgust.

"What?" said Claire as she read it. "What's the big deal?"

"The big deal," I told her, "is that I was *supposed* to get Nick. And here I end up with *Mia Malone*."

"Shh," went Claire, cutting her eyes quickly behind me.

I turned to see Mia strutting, nose up as usual, out the homeroom door.

I bit my lip, but she walked on and I was *pretty* sure she didn't hear me.

I sighed and shook my head. "My whole life is ruined." Then I looked down at *Claire*'s paper. "Or maybe not!"

Claire looked at it, too.

"Uh-uh," she said, letting her long, brown hair swing from side to side. "We can't switch. It's against the rules."

"What do you mean we can't switch? We're best friends."

"I know," said Claire. "But . . . we're not supposed to. We're not even supposed to tell each other who we have, you know."

I looked at her like, "Oh, come on!" I mean, this was a girl who stood up every day on the bus and was known to have "borrowed" her sister's makeup more than once. Since when had she worried so much about *rules*?

"Besides . . ." she went on — after glancing quickly around her. "I don't want Mia Malone either."

I nodded. "I know. I know. But I'll make it up to you, I promise. And really, it's only fair," I explained. "I mean, if I hadn't let you go ahead of me, *your* paper would have been mine to start with."

She smiled. "Oh, I see. . . ."

"You *know* how much I like him," I went on. "You just *have* to switch with me. *Please!*" Then, just to be sure, I asked her, "You do, um, have Nick, don't you?"

Her grin was answer enough.

"Okay, I'll do it," she said. "But you owe me big-time for this one!"

I could have cried (though I don't think I actually did that time), I was so happy. But it didn't last long. Because before our handoff was complete, up walked Ruby and Tallulah.

"What are you doing?" demanded Ruby.

"You're not switching Secret Santa names, are you?" said Tallulah.

This was typical nosy behavior for them, just so you know.

I looked at them. "None of your business."

"Well, it kind of is," Ruby replied. "Since we're in the same class and all."

"And it's definitely *Mrs. Bailey*'s business," Tallulah added, her arms crossed.

"Oh, come on," said Claire. "What do you care?"

Ruby crossed her arms so that they matched Tallulah's exactly, just like their Uggs, their silver purses, and the superlong scarves they'd taken to wearing with their *almost* matching sequined tops. It was hard to believe they couldn't stand each other last year.

"We care," said Ruby, "because it's, like, one of Mrs. Bailey's main rules."

"Totally," said Tallulah.

"And," Ruby went on, "because it's, like, not fair for you guys to trade when no one else is."

Tallulah nodded. "Like, not at all."

"Fine." Claire shrugged, turning confidently to me. "Like they'd really know if I'd gotten Nick to start with instead of you."

I know I winced as soon as she said it, though I'm not exactly sure if Tallulah and Ruby laughed or smirked.

"Oh my gosh!" squealed Ruby.

Tallulah's mouth fell. "Noel likes Nick!"

"No way!"

"Oh my gosh!"

I think I mumbled something like "Ring already, you dumb bell," and "Great, Claire. Thanks a lot."

"By the way," said Ruby, when she'd composed herself finally. "This is not a matchmaking exercise, you know."

"Like, not at all," said — yeah, you guessed it.

"But do whatever you want to. I mean, we *do* have an honor code, so I'll, like, *have* to tell Mrs. Bailey if you guys *do* switch names. . . ."

"But, yeah, do what you want to."

Then they readjusted their scarves and, with perfectly synchronized hair swings, turned and left us, still outside homeroom, the late bell clanging over my fuming head.

Claire put her arm around my sunken shoulder. "Sorry," she said somberly. "I guess you don't owe me one, after all."

If it's okay with you, I'd rather not get into the rest of the day in too much detail. Suffice it to say it was all pretty awful: got a C on my French quiz (as usual); had to redo my lab in earth science (not once, but three times); spilled spaghetti sauce on my sweater at lunch (I am never wearing anything white to school again); crashed into Isabelle playing basketball in gym (though she's the one who actually had to go to the nurse); and

22

had to sit there next to Nick in world civilization (no — of course *that* wasn't the bad part) while Tallulah and Ruby twittered and giggled two rows behind us (*that* was). I don't know what Nick was thinking — I couldn't even look at him all through class — but when we walked out his face was red and kind of intense and I was pretty sure he one hundred percent hated my guts.

I, of course, still liked him just as much — though I almost wished I didn't. Life is so much simpler when you aren't crushing on boys, you know? But sometimes you just can't help it — especially when they have eyes that are so blue they look like you might have colored them yourself and this shiny black hair that swoops down to hide their eyes almost every time they move. . . .

But it's not just that Nick's so cute, you know? He's really nice to everybody, too, and funny (without going *too* far all the time like other boys). Plus he's smart and really easy to talk to . . . or at least he was until Halloween, when we went trick-or-treating together. I mean, I thought we'd had fun. But ever since that night, it seemed he'd barely spoken to me. Maybe I should have been a Colts cheerleader instead of letting Claire talk me into being a toothbrush (she was the toothpaste). . . . I don't know.

At first, I kept trying to make conversation: Did you get that math homework? Are you going to the football game? But lately, I'd given up. It was too painful. He never said much. Which is why I'd thought being his Secret Santa would be so perfect! I could show him how much I liked him without even talking! And, hopefully, he'd realize I was really great and decide to like me back. . . . Life would be perfect. We'd live happily ever after. (Though I'd have to keep my maiden name; as Claire says, "Noel Holiday" is simply too much.)

Thanks to Tallulah and Ruby, however, this perfect plan was not to be. I mean, both Claire and I decided that switching names just wasn't worth it. We knew Ruby and Tallulah weren't just threatening. They would *definitely* tell. And Mrs. Bailey would be disappointed. And we liked her too much to do that. I guessed I'd just have to find some other way to get through to Nick . . . and in the meantime I'd have to suffer.

So I guess what I'm saying is I was kind of happy when the day was finally over and it was time, at last, to get on the bus and go home. Only thing is, I didn't get on the bus, because to make my day even more miserable, who but my very own mother should be waiting for me outside the school. And not in her car either. But right there out in the open where everyone in the whole world could see how absolutely ginormous she was.

"Hi, sweetie," she said.

"Mom," I groaned. "Why are you here?"

"Well," she said, "I was driving home from the doctor's and I thought it would be nice if I just went ahead and picked you and Cecee up. If that's okay with *you*, of course."

No! I thought to myself. *It certainly is not.* My day was already bad enough. The last thing I needed was everybody staring openmouthed at my freak show of a mother, so pregnant that even my dad's old overcoat couldn't completely cover her up.

And, frankly, if you asked me, her sarcasm wasn't called for either.

"Oh, fine," I muttered. "Let's go." I thought, *Before you attract too much attention.*

"Hi, Mrs. Moore! How are you feeling?"

We turned, and there was Claire, grinning and slipping on her gloves.

"Pretty good, considering. Thanks," my mom said. "Only a few more weeks to go."

"Is it kicking much?" Claire asked her.

My mother shook her head. "Not much right now, but you're welcome to try to feel for something if you want."

She smiled and pulled back the sides of her coat to make a place for Claire's hand on her stomach. Claire loved to feel the baby, every chance she got. But I was way, way over it. It was cool in the beginning, I guess, but now it scared me, frankly . . . the thought of something trapped inside there, completely alive and kicking and punching and rolling around. What would it be like when it came out? Why couldn't it just be still?

"Ooh, there! I think I feel it!" Claire exclaimed. "Noel, want to try?"

"No thanks," I said, stepping back toward the parking lot. "Come on, Mom. Don't we have to go?"

"I suppose we do," she said. She reached out to give Claire the closest thing to a hug that she could, considering. "I'd offer to take you home, Claire," she said, "but we still have to pick up Cecee and stop at the grocery store."

"No problem," Claire told her. "See you tomorrow," she said to me. "We'll do our Secret Santa shopping?"

"Yeah." I nodded. "Sounds good. I'll call you in the morning."

I hurried to the car, leaving my mom to waddle along behind me.

"Secret Santa?" she said as she opened the door and worked to wedge herself in behind the steering wheel. "That sounds fun!"

"It's not fun," I said. I paused to help her with her seat belt. "It's schoolwork. It's something we have to do for homeroom. And though it could have been fun, it won't be."

"Why not?" asked my mom.

"Mom," I muttered. "I don't want to talk about it."

"I see. . . ."

We drove down past the high school and into our neighborhood, where my old school — now Cecee's school — is. My mom pulled up to the curb just as the first graders were coming out.

"Hmm." She cut off the engine and sighed. "Noel, hon, could you go get her? I'm just not up to battling with this steering wheel again."

From my mom's pursed-lip reaction I think it's highly likely I made a do-I-really-*have*-to face.

"Do I really *have* to?" I asked her.

She looked at me.

"Oh, okay."

I emerged from the warmth of the car and hurried up the sidewalk to the schoolyard. It was windy and kind of cloudy, the first really *cold* day of the winter, and I could tell it was time to lose the vest when I got home and mount a closet expedition for my big down coat. Happily, though, my feet were doing okay.

You see, I'd decided that my "look" this year would be "surfer-girl," which, as far as I was concerned, meant Roxy shorts until Thanksgiving, and Vans — without socks — for the whole, entire year. (And no, no matter what Claire may say, it had absolutely nothing to do with Nick's declaring that he is into surfing this year. Pure coincidence, this, I swear.) Any other winter I know my mom would have been convinced I'd catch pneumonia — but the one *good* thing about the new baby was that it kept her mind busy with a million other things.

By the time I got to Cecee, she was standing surrounded by a circle of adoring friends. I could tell she was regaling them, as usual, with some outrageous story — complete with lots of dramatic hand waves — which elicited several bursts of giggles and rounds of high-pitched "Oh, Cecee! No way!"s.

My little sister, I should probably tell you, is much cooler than I am. I'm totally serious. Six going on sixteen, as my dad always likes to say — well on the road to fabulous adulthood, without those awkward adolescent speed bumps slowing her down along the way. She even looks like a miniature grown-up — with my mom's thick, wavy hair and long, dark lashes, and that way they both have of standing with their hips out, like supermodels. (Though my mom hadn't been doing *that* for a few months, you know.)

Oh, and get this: Here Cecee is in first grade, and she gets more phone calls than I do! I'm actually glad there's six years between us. It means I'll never have to compete with her in the same school. She'd blow me away!

So anyway, I get there and right away notice that not only was Cecee dressed all in her new favorite color, black, but that beneath their puffy pink and purple snow jackets almost every other girl in her class was, too. (This happened before, I should tell you, back in September, with brown.) *Like lemmings,* I thought. *It's disgusting.* (And why, exactly, was it that it never happened to me?)

"Noel!" she cried out as soon as she saw me. "Look! It's my sister, everybody! Here, take my backpack. Noel! Noel!" She ran up and sacked me with a hug.

Did I also mention she's pretty sweet?

"Can I have a playdate today? Can I? *Please?*" She stood back and her face fell into a business-like expression. "Caitlin and Madison *need* for me to give them makeovers." Then she grinned. "Hey! I could do you, too, *finally!*"

Did I say sweet? I was mistaken.

I shook my head. "Nope. No way. Mom's got to go to the store."

"Aww!" She pouted. "Too bad." Then she turned to her admirers. "Gotta go shopping with my *big* sister," she said with a compassionate, too-bad-for-you-poor-suckers shrug. "But I'll definitely talk with my mother and schedule makeover times for *everyone.*" She gave each one a hug and an air kiss, then held her hand up to her ear. "Don't forget to call me!"

"Um, don't you have to tell your teacher you're going now?" I said in what I thought was my best, all-knowing, big-sister way.

Cecee looked at me, however, like I'd proposed a diaper change.

"Noel!" she howled. "That is, like, so kindergarten!" Then she turned to her friends and they *all* laughed like crazy. (It's a sad day, I will tell you, when a bunch of little first graders make you feel completely dumb.)

So I did what I had to: I reached out and grabbed her hand and dragged her off to the car.

"How was middle school?" she asked as she happily skipped along.

Of course, I hardly felt like admitting it couldn't possibly get any worse.

"Well, in *first* grade, Milo Dodd farted," she said, and I think I laughed out loud.

Well, maybe it could.

❄CHAPTER THREE❄

The next day I hit the mall to do Secret Santa shopping with Claire. And I've got to say that by the time we got there, I was feeling much better about the whole thing. So what if I had Mia and not Nick? Big deal. It could still be fun. It wasn't just about who I had, after all. It was about who had me, as well!

I knew Claire didn't have me. (Too bad!) But maybe Olivia or Isabelle did. Or — and how awesome would this be — maybe even Nick! *Uh-oh,* I thought. I sure wished I had thought to clear my locker of anything embarrassing on Friday! Oh, well. . . .

We strolled into Target and grabbed two carts and rode them, scooter-style, to the holiday aisle to begin.

"*Aw!* How cute is *this*?" said Claire. She picked up a roll of Santa-kitten-covered paper. "Don't you love it!"

"It's cute," I said. "But . . . maybe too cute for a boy. Besides, I'm not *sure* that Nick really likes cats." (Fact: I knew it, for sure.)

I spotted another roll with snowmen playing hockey on it. "Now *this* is more like it. Don't you think?"

"Totally. Cool."

She put the snowman roll in her basket and handed the kitten one to me. "Use it for Mia," she said.

It *was* cute. . . . "Okay."

Then we each grabbed some ribbon and bows, along with garlands, silver tinsel, and bags of tiny jingle bells.

"Do you think," said Claire as she surveyed our collection, "our ten-dollar limit is supposed to include decorations, too?"

I stared and sighed. "Good question." Then I shrugged. "If it's too much, we'll put some back and share."

Problem solved, we moved on to the candy aisle, where Claire (who's a chocoholic) went for the Hershey's kisses right away.

"Uh, *excuse* me," I said, returning the bag to

where it came from. "But you weren't *really* going to give kisses to the guy *I* like, were you?"

"Oh . . . right." Claire blushed. "Sorry. How 'bout M&M's?"

I nodded and said, "That's fine. Oh, and get peanut. He's crazy about those."

He'd bought them constantly from the vending machine at the pool all summer long. Me, I'm a plain girl. But that didn't mean I didn't buy the peanut kind all summer, too — to share with him, of course!

As for Mia, who *knew* what she liked? Probably truffles, or something gourmet and expensive like that. Well — I grabbed a bag of peanut M&M's myself — with a ten-dollar budget, she'd just have to settle, I guessed.

"Candy canes?" Claire asked me.

"But of course," I said.

Our baskets looked full already. But there was still a lot more to get . . . and let me tell you, Claire needed my help badly. I mean, she almost got Nick a little Patriots notebook and a game of Harry Potter Uno that was on sale.

"No, no, no," I told her. "These things won't do at all. First of all, he hates the Patriots." I traded that notebook in for one with the horseshoe instead. "He likes the Colts."

"Okay," Claire said. "But I could have sworn he liked Harry Potter."

"He *did*," I explained. "Not so much anymore."

Not since he'd finished the seventh book this summer, also at the pool.

"Okay," Claire said. "So what *should* I get him, do you think?"

"Easy," I said. "Follow me."

I led her to the toy section, where we found a cheap harmonica to replace the one he'd lost on our class overnight in September. It wasn't half as nice, I knew. But he was really good and I was sure that he could make it sound okay.

"And then maybe some bubble gum," I told Claire. "Something sour, not too sweet."

Then I stopped.

"Hold on. What am I doing?!"

Claire asked, "What do you mean?"

"I mean, I don't know why I'm helping you. Even if you *don't* give him kisses, when Nick finds out *you* gave him all this stuff, he still could think *you* like him."

"Well, I don't," Claire said, laughing.

"*I* know," I said. "But *he* won't. And he might think you're so great he'll start liking *you* back . . . like he *should* be doing with me."

"Oh, Noel. You're crazy. And remember, we're

supposed to give things that are meaningful and special."

"Maybe," I said. "But still . . . maybe put the Colts thing and the harmonica back . . . or . . . keep the Colts thing . . . but definitely put the harmonica back. . . ."

"Are you sure?" Claire asked.

"Yeah . . . I think."

"Okay, so how 'bout a Rudolph nose and a Santa hat instead?"

"Perfect!" I said. "Claire, I love you!"

But, of course, our job wasn't done when Nick's list was filled. We still had to finish Mia's. But what do you get for someone that you hardly know at all? We wandered around the store for a while, hoping for inspiration. But it failed to come.

I lingered, as I always do, in the arts-and-crafts department and considered for a second getting some fun yarn and knitting Mia a scarf. I'd learned how to knit back in fifth grade and liked to do it (though I never seem to have the time to make all the things I'd like to).

But then I thought maybe "homemade" was not Mia Malone's thing. After all, no matter how careful I was, there was always a little something in the stuff I knitted that gave its humble origins away, and I shuddered at the thought of Mia looking down her stuck-up nose at something I'd gone to all the trouble to make.

"Yeah, it's not worth the chance, I guess," agreed Claire. "But you can make one for me anytime!"

I smiled. *Gift idea for Claire for Christmas,* I thought to myself. *Consider it done.*

"Ooh, look!" she exclaimed. She'd stopped in front of the display at the end of the knitting aisle. "Look at all this *baby* yarn. Oh, feel how soft it is."

She rubbed a skein against her cheek and handed another one to me. It was delicate and downy, less like yarn and more like fluffy, sherbet-colored air.

"Have you made anything for the baby yet?" she asked me.

"No" was all I said. I didn't get into all the details of how much the baby had already — all the mountains of blankets and clothes and fancy dust rags that my mother called "burp cloths" that kept pouring in from aunts and neighbors, not to mention the ancient stuff of mine and Cecee's my mom had never seen fit to give away. That baby didn't need anything else, especially something made by me.

"Well, you should!" Claire told me.

"Yeah, I guess. Maybe. But not today. Why don't we just go back to the holiday section," I suggested, "and get whatever girly, Christmassy stuff they have back there."

There was plenty, that was for sure.

My personal favorites were the earrings, especially the candy canes and reindeer.

"Ooh! I want these so *bad*!" I told Claire, holding up the long candy-cane ones and letting them dangle beside my ear.

"I know!" she said. "They're so cute!"

But did *Mia* have pierced ears? we wondered. We couldn't remember, but it seemed likely, so I tossed them into the cart.

Some peppermint lip gloss was, of course, a no-brainer. She did have *lips,* we knew, after all. And a big red bow headband. Very cute. A jingle-bell bracelet; that seemed fun. And a long, fuzzy pen with a googly-eyed elf on top . . .

"Well, hi, guys!"

Claire and I both looked up to see who else but Ruby and Tallulah.

"Secret Santa shopping, I see."

I nodded to Ruby. "Uh-huh. You too?"

"Yep."

"Totally," added Tallulah.

I eyed the cart that they were sharing (Come on, I couldn't help it. I mean, it was right there in front of me.) and noted their festive load: Santa paper and lots of bows (of course) and packs of little chocolate Santas, long chains of tiny candy canes, an adorable little bear wearing a scarf that said MERRY CHRISTMAS, plus a very cute pair of mistletoe earrings, Hershey kisses, and one of those magnets shaped like a license plate that had the name COLE. . . .

Cole! *No way,* I thought. That was who *Ruby* had a crush on!

"Who has Cole?" I asked. "Is it *you*?"

Ruby tried, but couldn't help smiling.

"You know I can't tell you," she said.

But she didn't have to. I turned to Claire.

"Can you believe it?" I said. "Here she goes making this big deal of my trying to get Nick — who I may or may *not* like, by the way," I paused to inform them. "And all the time she has who *she* likes!"

"Hey," Ruby spoke up. "This is different! This is fate."

"Yeah, right," I mumbled. Fate, my foot!

"No, it totally was," Tallulah agreed, almost guiltily pulling their shopping cart behind her.

Ruby, meanwhile, lifted her arms apologetically. "Hey, if I got Cole — and I'm not saying I *did* — I guess it's because it was just meant to be." She grinned. "I'd never break Mrs. Bailey's rules," she went on, staring at me. "And you better not either."

"Don't worry," said Claire, "we're *not*."

"Good."

Yeah, I thought. *Great.*

"Hey, Ruby," said Tallulah. "Don't you think we should keep shopping?" She nodded to their cart and raised her eyebrows.

"Oh yeah," Ruby said. "Okay." She turned to join Tallulah, and with "ta-ta" waves they continued on their way.

"You know," said Claire once we were sure they were aisles away, "she *could* be telling the truth. She could have gotten Cole just by chance yesterday."

"Yeah, I guess," I told her. "It's just . . . it's so not fair."

Still, running into Ruby and Tallulah had not been all that bad. . . . Sure, they had a bunch of stuff for Cole, but they also had some pretty awesome stuff — for whoever Tallulah had. And from the way she was guarding their cart, the odds were pretty good, I thought, that it was one of us!

"So are we ready, you think?" Claire asked me, giving her own cart a little turn. She looked down at the earrings I was still holding in my hand. "I mean . . . you don't really want to get those for yourself still, do you?"

"Nah," I said, smiling — I'm sure — as I put them back. "And if we can't spend more than ten dollars, then, yeah, I think we're through."

It was actually going to be fun, I realized, to fix up someone's locker and surprise them — even Mia. And it was *really* going to be fun to see who surprised me.

For the first time in my whole life, I think I was actually looking forward to Monday morning.

❄C❄HAPTER F❄OUR❄

It wasn't easy, but Claire and I were at school Monday morning the *second* the doors opened. It was still dark out and my dad was still in his pajamas, but my mom told him that no child should be discouraged from getting to school early instead of late (and that he was crazy if he thought *she* was going to drive us).

Mr. Kochar, the janitor, let us in with a glance at his watch and a startled "Hello."

"Good morning," we said. "Happy Monday."

"Class assignment," I explained. "You know."

After all, we had to get to school before any-one else did, to make sure we had time to do our Secret Santas without getting caught.

We waited for Mr. Kochar to open the stairwell,

then hurried up to the second floor to do Nick's locker first.

No one else was up there, not even the teachers, and it was eerily quiet, like a horror movie, kind of. I couldn't help it — I had to let Claire walk ahead of me, then run up and grab her shoulders.

"Ahh-h-h-h-h!"

We both screamed, then started to laugh.

"Do not do that again!" she warned me.

"Promise," I said. "Sorry."

"Where's the light switch, anyway?" she asked.

I found it and flipped it on and in a few seconds, after the bulbs kicked in, the hall was flooded with its usual get-to-work, we're-watching-you light.

"That's more like it," said Claire.

She opened her purse and fished around for a second, then pulled out Nick's crumpled paper.

"Let's see . . ." she said. "Locker 2245 . . ."

We walked down the hall, past the science labs, toward homeroom, on the opposite side from where Claire's and my lockers were.

"Here it is!" I said. (I'd known it all along, of course.)

"Okay," said Claire. She switched the paper to her left hand and reached for the locker door.

I beat her to it, then stopped and smiled. "Can I do it?" I begged her. *"Please?"*

Claire shrugged. "Okay with me . . ." She winked. "Just don't tell Ruby."

I rolled my eyes.

"Okay, ready? Six . . . thirty-eight . . . eighteen . . ."

"Hold on," I said, all flustered. "Let me start again." Can you believe my hand was shaking? Embarrassing, right? I know!

At last, though, I managed to get it right and get it open, and there we stood before Nick Holiday's very own locker. It was almost, I thought, like staring into his very soul. . . .

Except, not really — unless his soul was very messy (which I seriously doubt).

Let's see. . . . There were lots of textbooks, three copies of *one* — I think it was history — in fact; a whole binder's worth of loose-leaf paper, crumpled and scattered about; a few library books, including some fantasy I'd never heard of, a biography of Peyton Manning, and a book of popular harmonica songs; a crushed paper bag that we highly suspected contained an extremely old lunch; a mass of dark, thick sweatshirts; a football and a skateboard and six or seven gloves, each one looking for a mate . . . I sighed. How perfect; they were just like us!

The inside of the door was *covered* with stickers, some put there by Nick, but some left over from past years, I was sure. There were skateboard ones, and some from surf shops, and some blue Colts horseshoes, too, plus the whole cast of *High School Musical* . . . with drawn-on mustaches and beards.

"Maybe we should clean it for him?" I suggested to Claire.

"You're kidding, right?" she said, staring at me in horror.

I laughed as if I had been. (Though I'd been as serious as a French test.)

Claire surveyed the scene and sighed. "Hmm . . . I feel like I should have gotten him that harmonica, after all."

"I know," I said, feeling sorry we hadn't, as well. "Maybe for Friday . . ."

"Yeah . . . well, I should get started, I guess."

She pulled the wrapping paper out of her bag, along with some scissors, and set the rest down.

"Yeah, me too."

Some teachers had started arriving and, as I glanced at the hall clock, I knew it wouldn't be long before students started coming in, too.

"Meet me in the bathroom," I told her, "after you're done and I'm done with Mia's."

45

Then I carried my own bag, along with my backpack, back down the hall and down the stairs to the first floor.

Wow, I thought to myself as I neared the 1100 row. I hadn't been in *that* hall since last year. I guess that's what you get when you start school a month late — a locker all by yourself, with the sixth grade and that's about it.

Too bad for her, I thought.

I found Mia's locker pretty easily, since it was just two away from my old one. Good old 1140. I stopped and tried my old combination, just to see if it still worked, but nothing happened so I moved on. They probably change them every year. Makes sense, I guess.

I stopped at 1142 and set down my sack full of Santa supplies. I figured it would be best to decorate the outside of the locker first — since it could easily take the longest — so I unrolled a long piece of wrapping paper and carefully cut it to fit the door.

I am not the best present wrapper at *all,* but I did a fairly good job on Mia's locker, I must admit. The kittens were nice and straight — and right-side up, I'm happy to say. And after I taped one long ribbon from top to bottom, and another from side to side, and stuck a bow where they crossed in the middle, the door looked just like a giant gift you'd have to be crazy not to want to open.

"Oh, how nice, Noel," said Ms. Kelso, my sixth-grade English teacher, as she walked by.

"Thanks," I told her.

"But aren't Secret Santas for Mrs. Bailey's *seventh* grade friends?" she said.

(Don't ask me why, please, but for some reason she has this thing about calling kids "friends.")

"They are," I told her, nodding. "This friend just started late," I explained.

"Ah," she replied, smiling. "Well, good. So nice to see you again."

"You too, Ms. Kelso. See ya."

I waved her on to her room in the corner, then turned back to Mia's locker, and with a steady hand this time, dialed the combination and opened it up.

It was, and I'm not kidding, the most boring locker I'd ever seen.

I mean, especially for a girl! No noteboard. No wallpaper. No mirror. No nothing but two books and some pictures taped to the inside of the door.

I looked at them closely. (After all, that was our assignment, was it not?) There were several school-picture-looking photos of boys and girls I didn't know, all with neat hair and those weird

47

school-picture smiles that always look too stiff or just too wild. Plus more of what looked like the same kids all together and having fun. At the beach. In a bowling alley. On some bleachers holding a sign that said GO CARDINALS!

It actually took me a minute to realize that Mia was among them. I mean, I'm not sure I'd ever even seen her smile before, and trust me, it changed her face completely. No kidding. She looked like a different person in the pictures. Happy. Fun-loving. Friendly . . .

I remember thinking she was either faking it *there,* or not the girl I thought she was at my school at all. . . .

But I didn't have much time to wonder about it, really, because the next thing I knew, a pack of sixth graders had me surrounded.

"Ohh! That's so pretty!" several told me.

"What are you doing?" one of them asked.

"Do mine, too!" another demanded.

I turned around and sighed. "Sorry," I said kindly. "It's a seventh-grade thing, you see."

Then, seeing how late it was getting, I hurried to finish my job. (It was easy, let me tell you, with the locker so totally empty.) First I hung a candy cane on each one of the hooks, along with some jingle bells and lots of silver tinsel. Then

I draped shiny garlands all around the locker, and taped them all over the inside of the door. Finally, up on the shelf with Mia's books, I put the bag of M&M's and a fancy holiday card someone had sent to my house but conveniently forgotten to sign.

I didn't write much in it, just:

Surprise!

From your Secret Santa

But I figured that was enough. And the locker was an absolute masterpiece, I thought, if I did say so myself. (And of course I did.)

I shut the door proudly and smiled at my sixth-grade fan club, then I hurried off to the bathroom to meet up with Claire.

"How's it look?" Claire asked me as we stood, sharing my brush, in front of our usual mirrors.

"Awesome," I said, "of course." (Mia's locker. Not my hair.)

My hair was hopeless, as usual, and made even worse by the fact that I hadn't had time that morning to take a shower. Oh, well. I tried to do what I could for it . . . then gave up and surrendered to a good old ponytail.

"Did you see anyone else doing lockers? And do you have a headband?" I asked Claire.

"Sorry, no. And yeah, I did." She bent her head forward, brushed her hair over, then dramatically flipped it back. It looked really good. Then she did it again.

"Who?" I asked her.

"Isabelle . . . and Olivia."

"Nick," I asked, "by any chance?"

She smiled at me. "No. Not him."

"Ruby and Tallulah?"

"No, not them either . . . and not *Cole* . . . oh, but I did see Mia."

"Really?" I said, interested. "Whose locker does she have?"

"I don't know. She was just getting there as I left. She walked right by me, but she didn't say anything, of course."

"Of course." I nodded. Like always. "Man." I rolled my eyes. "This must be absolute *torture* for her. She actually has to interact with us. The horror!"

Claire laughed. "Poor thing. Oh! And speaking of horror — did you start your history paper yet?"

I made a face into the mirror — basically *ugh!* with a *don't even ask!*

Not all teachers, you see, had Mrs. Bailey's holiday spirit. Madame Greenwood's gift to us, for instance, was replacing our end-of-the-week

French quiz with a grand exam. (Word to the wise: Do not take French in the seventh grade unless you absolutely have to!) While Mr. Menendez was expecting five whole pages (single-spaced, no less) on an Indian holiday of our own choosing. Claire had picked Diwali, the festival of lights; I hadn't even decided yet.

"No," I told her grimly. Though I'd meant to. Honestly.

Not on Saturday, of course. I hung out at Claire's for most of the day. But I'd fully intended on working on Sunday. Unfortunately, the day didn't go quite as I planned.

It should have been easy: Get up, go to church, then go get a tree and decorate it, then have the rest of the day to myself. No big deal, right? Think again.

The whole tree thing was just a mess! First of all, my dad refused to let my mom help at all "in her condition." So who got to help him load the beast onto and off of the car? As Madame Greenwood would say, *moi!* And I hate to say it, but I'm just not that strong. It took a good half hour just to get it from the car through the front door.

And then the decorating! *Ahhh!* (That's an ear-piercing, desperate scream, by the way.)

Now, we usually have a system. My mom does the lights, then Cecee and I put on all the decorations. My dad makes the popcorn and we all have a jolly time.

But of course *this* year Dad tells my mom, "No way! You're not getting on a ladder." And he decides to do the lights himself, with my mom on the couch for moral support and "suggestions."

Naturally, it was a disaster.

"No, not that way! What are you doing? They're all bunched on the bottom! I can see the cords. That looks awful."

These were just a few of my mom's helpful "suggestions," the result of which was that my dad stormed off to watch the football game on the TV in the bedroom. Meanwhile, my mom had me help her bring all the ornaments down from the attic, which resulted in *her* declaring that it was time for *us* to "clean up this horrific mess."

The entire attic. I am not kidding. It took the rest of the afternoon.

By the time we were done cleaning a place that, if you ask me, was *designed* to be messy, my dad had emerged and finished stringing the lights, and my mom's mood was much improved.

"Come see what we did!" she told my dad. "I guess I've started *nesting*." (Whatever that means.)

And so, while they went, hand in hand, to inspect the unnecessarily orderly attic, I was left to hang all ten boxes' worth of ornaments on the tree all by myself.

But what about Cecee? you might ask. *Where in the world was she?*

Good question. Here's the answer: running around the house, toting my old baby doll, with a blue pillowcase on her head.

She was "rehearsing," so she said, for next week's Christmas pageant at church, in which she would be playing . . . who else? You guessed it. Mary.

Now, I know that I'm nearly thirteen and way too old for pageants and things . . . but really, come on! Is it odd to think it unfair that my little sister gets the best part of all, when all I ever got to be were shepherds . . . oh yeah, and a *sheep* one year.

"Aren't you going to help me?" I asked her.

"Sorry, Noel," she told me. "I only have a week to get this right, you know," she said.

"You know, that's *my* doll," I said bitterly as she laid it in the cat's bed. "Why don't you use your own?"

She smiled up at me, her hands by her chin, straight up and down and flat together. "Yours looks poorer. More like Jesus," she beneficently explained. "Ooh! But if Mom had her baby right now, I could use it instead!"

"Clearly, you don't know *anything* about babies," I said. "And if you're not going to help me, I wish you'd find another stable." I'm sure I glared at her. "And could I at least have a little popcorn down here?" I yelled.

"Sorry, hon," my mom hollered back. "We're out. I'll get more tomorrow."

By dinnertime, I was starving *and* exhausted.

Unfortunately, I didn't have time to explain *any* of this to Claire on Monday morning because the next thing I knew, the first bell of the morning was sounding from the hall.

"Eight-thirty already?"

We looked at each other. Boy, time really flies when you're trying to look good.

I rubbed some lip balm on my lips — which I had sworn to myself not to let get chapped again this winter. Then we exited the girls' room. Homeroom was to the right, but I pulled Claire the other way.

"Don't you want to check out our lockers real quick?" I asked her.

She grabbed my hands. "Of course! Okay!"

We hurried down to the section where our lockers were — and it looked utterly amazing! Now *this* was what Christmas was about!

Nick's locker, I noticed immediately, looked absolutely awesome (Good call there with the hockey snowmen, thank you very much!), as did Claire's now, and lots of others — and the hall was filled with kids *ooh*ing and *ahh*ing, as some yanked doors open and squealed with glee.

My locker, on the other hand, looked horribly, glaringly, painfully plain.

At least on the outside.

The second bell rang and Claire tugged on my arm to pull me away to class, but I just couldn't go yet. I reached for the lock.

4–24–14.

Click. Creak. Open.

Nope. Nothing.

Hmm?

Oh, well . . . I thought. *That's okay.* Apparently, my Secret Santa was waiting till later in the day. Maybe they couldn't get to school early that morning. Besides, it was a good thing, I decided, since I'd forgotten to take my gym suit home on Friday. Gross. I picked it up off the floor of my locker and shoved it into my backpack.

Okay now, I thought, *Secret Santa, this locker's all yours!*

❄ CHAPTER FIVE ❄

It's not easy to say this, but by lunch my locker still had not been touched, and as you can imagine, I was beginning to get a little bummed.

Okay, I'll admit it: I'd been bummed out of my mind since second period.

I mean, now not only did I have to listen to everyone go on and on about their fabulous holiday plans, I had to hear about their awesome Secret Santas, too — *still* with nothing to contribute of my own.

"Can you believe how many candy canes I got?!" said Olivia. "Here, everyone take one. Aren't they cute!"

"Check out all this *gelt!*" said Isabelle. "I wonder if my Secret Santa's Jewish, too?" She smiled at Dustin and Josh especially. "Here, have some, *please*. If I eat it all I'm going to be absolutely sick!!"

Lunch, in fact, turned into a veritable candy swap — with some homemade Santa cookies thrown in. (Those came from Mason ... *begrudgingly*.) And I've got to say, I felt like a beggar with nothing of my own to add. I mean, if someone offered me something and said, "And what did *you* get?" again, I was positively sure I would scream! (Of course they did, but I kept my cool and said simply, "Uh ... nothing yet ... sorry," and accepted their looks of pity and their charity with the utmost grace.)

The only person who didn't seem totally psyched with their locker booty was Nick — to Claire's and my complete surprise.

"I thought he loved peanut M&M's," said Claire, as we watched him solemnly distribute them at the boys' end of the table.

"Well, he used to," I told her.

"I guess we don't have to worry about him falling in love with his Secret Santa," she said, shrugging.

Yeah, I thought kind of sadly. *I guess not.*

Cole, on the other hand, was ga-ga over his own Secret Santa. "I mean, I love Hershey's Kisses!" he went on ... and on.

I glanced at Ruby, who was practically *dying* as Tallulah helped her straighten her new mistletoe earrings. Yeah, I probably made a face at her. I mean, really. Come on!

There was, of course, one other person from homeroom not participating in the great swap — though I wasn't sure exactly if that made me happy or not. It was Mia, who was, as always, sitting off at another table all alone. She was eating her usual sack lunch and reading her usual book and did not seem, as far as I could tell, to have *her* candy with her at all.

Hmph. Oh, well. Whatever.

"Don't worry," said Claire as she lifted Santa's head and squeezed me out a lemon PEZ. "Everyone got a Secret Santa. You'll get yours, too. You just have to be patient, I guess."

And I tried. I really did.

I totally waited for each bell to ring before fleeing class to check my locker. But every time I found it just the same.

That is, till sixth period.

That's when I rounded the corner to see my Secret Santa's handiwork . . . a teeny-tiny *broken* candy cane taped to the front of my locker door.

What? I thought. *Was this some kind of heinous joke?*

Was I being punked?!

I looked around at all the other lockers, all wrapped up in bright paper and shiny, happy, stupid bows. Sure, some were messier than others, and some were a little too tinselly for me . . . but I would have taken *any* of them over what I got!

I hurried to yank the candy cane off before, hopefully, anyone else could see. After all, don't you think it's better to have *nothing* than the lamest Secret Santa in the whole, entire school?

Honestly, I was so upset, I could hardly get my locker open. I mean, my hand was shaking more than when I'd dialed Nick's combination. When I finally did open it, I tossed in some books, grabbed some others plus my coat, and quickly looked at myself in my mirror, telling myself, "Don't you dare cry!"

Then I slammed it shut and, well, I'll just go ahead and say it: I totally ran away.

I know. I know. I was overreacting — maybe. But it all just seemed so unfair! *Why me?* I wondered. Why should the one person with such bad holiday luck already get stuck with the worst Secret Santa in the whole entire world? Hmm? Tell me that. And don't think I didn't have my suspicions of who my Santa was, either. Think the most clueless, humorless, friendless, antisocial person in homeroom. You got it: Mia.

"Maybe not," said Claire later when we talked on the phone. "Maybe you just got someone who didn't have enough time today."

"How does one person out of twenty not have enough time?" I asked her. "I mean, we all have basically the same schedule, don't we? And, I mean, it's like an *assignment*. What kind of psycho just blows it off?"

"There's gotta be some logical explanation," Claire assured me. "Like you said, it is an assignment. Even someone as out of it as Mia is not just going to not *do* it."

"I don't know," I told her. "Remember, she didn't want to do it in the first place."

"Yeah, I guess," said Claire, "but I still think you should just wait till tomorrow. And don't worry," she added. "If you still don't get anything, I promise to share what I get with you."

"Thanks," I muttered. "Hey, hold on. It's my call waiting. . . ."

I knew who it was, of course, already.

"Hey, Claire. Sorry. It's Cecee's friend. I *know*. But she's been hovering around me for, like, an hour now. I'll call you back later. Bye. Hey, Cecee!"

I called. "Swaddle your — I mean *my* — doll and get the phone!"

Then, what else could I do? I shut myself up in my room and stewed.

The next day I went to school buoyed by the happy thought that some great tragedy had befallen my Secret Santa yesterday . . . but that today all would be well and good with him/her and the world.

I would *not* assume the worst of my *own* Santa-ee, Mia. No. I would, like Santa himself, give her the benefit of the doubt.

I got there early again with Claire — though not quite as early as the day before — and left her to do Nick's locker while I went down to see to Mia's.

The halls were lit, at least, and most of the teachers were there already, but I was happy to have the hall pretty much to myself again. It is nice to be in school when it is quiet and peaceful and your own. You feel like you own the place, you know — almost like it's a second home. Except for late at night, of course, like that one time I had to go to the bathroom during last year's spring show. I swear, it felt like the set of a horror movie. I'll never do that again alone!

61

Anyway, I quickly found Mia's locker (the only one down there decorated, of course) and dialed her combination, and I've got to say when I opened it up I was a little surprised to see a couple of things: One — though one candy cane was missing, the peanut M&M's did not look as if they'd been touched; and two — all the stuff I'd hung on the inside of the door was gone! No paper. No garlands. Just a few curly ribbons running drearily down the sides.

What was with that? I wondered. What kind of person doesn't like M&M's or decorations? She'd left the front intact, thank goodness. But it all seemed very odd.

Still, that wasn't my problem. I had a job to do. In fact now, I realized, I had a challenge. I suddenly decided I wasn't just going to be Mia's Secret Santa — I was going to be the absolute best Secret Santa she could ever hope to have! I'd make it so she couldn't just dismiss me or this project. I'd make her see that the kids at Northern Middle School couldn't be ignored!

And who knew . . . ? If she *was* my Secret Santa, I might hopefully inspire her! (Or at least make her feel miserably guilty for completely ruining my life.)

I was glad I still had all my Santa supplies with me because I quickly went to work doing her locker all over again, this time covering the inside *completely* with paper and ribbons and basically everything I had left. Then I not only hung a dozen more candy canes and perched the M&M's more prominently, I hung *all* the things I'd gotten her from her hooks. The lip gloss. Some stickers. The pen. Even the earrings that I loved and *almost* decided to keep for myself the night before. (I mean, if no one *else* was going to give me some . . .)

There, Mia, I thought, wiping my hands with satisfaction. *Take that!*

"Wow!" said a sixth grader, sneaking behind me and making me jump. "That looks amazing!"

"Thanks," I said. I turned around and took a bow.

There had never in school history been such a great Secret Santa, I was sure. To be so generous, so selfless, especially considering *I* hadn't received anything but a dumb little candy cane yet. At least, not as of yesterday.

But what about today?

I slammed the locker shut and ran to the second floor to check.

❄ Chapter Six ❄

My locker did not look promising as I approached it from the stairs — not even a candy cane taped to it. *Too bad,* I thought, still tasting the plate full of sausage I'd wolfed down for breakfast that morning, I could have used it.

I let my backpack slide to the floor with a thump and gave my locker a sullen kick, then — casting a quick look at my classmates cheerfully digging into theirs — I opened it up.

Please! I pleaded. *Please! Please let there be something in my locker this morning! Please let my Secret Santa have gotten her act together today!*

Then I looked — and there it was! I mean, I couldn't have missed it, sitting there gleaming like a big, silver (rectangular) star, right on top of my algebra book: a shiny silver envelope with

SURPRISE! written in gold ink across the front. I grabbed it and tore it open and laughed as a fountain of metallic confetti literally came pouring out.

Then I read the card:

HAPPY HOLIDAYS!

YOU ARE MOST CORDIALLY INVITED TO CLAIRE FULLER'S

SECOND ANNUAL CAROLING PARTY!

FRIDAY, DECEMBER 20TH

6:00–?

TACOS AND HOT CHOCOLATE TO BE SERVED.

DRESS WARMLY!

RSVP TO CLAIRE

Oh, I thought. *Fun . . . I guess.*

But was that all?

I scoured my locker, pulling out books and papers and anything that wasn't bolted down, searching for something, anything even remotely resembling a gift or thoughtful, secret surprise. . . .

In a minute, I had a floor full of locker guts . . . and that's about all.

"Hi," said Claire. "Did you get my invitation? I wanted to surprise you! Er . . . what's going on?"

"I can't believe it," I choked. My fists were all clenched, though I'm not exactly sure if I was mad or sad or what.

"*What?*" Claire asked, worried. Then she peeked into my locker. "Still no Secret Santa?"

I chewed my lip and heaved a sigh.

"Oh . . . that's too bad. But look," she went on, "my Secret Santa hasn't come yet this morning either."

I jammed my earthly possessions back into my locker and shook my head. "But you know they *will*," I muttered. "You know they're not some stuck-up snob with no intention of doing anything, ever. What's the point of this stupid assignment anyway?" I went on. "I'm going to write a letter to the school board and demand that it be stopped!"

"Well, let's tell Mrs. Bailey first," Claire said, rational, as always. "She can make some announcement, or something. . . . She won't let you get left out like this. Even if she has to be your Secret Santa herself!" She gave me a chin-up smile as she carefully set the jar of pins I've been collecting since sixth grade back on my shelf.

I probably have at least eighty — or maybe a hundred pins by now. I used to wear different ones every day, usually mixing some cute ones, like Hello Kitty, with more punk ones like skulls and bones and "Say 'No' to fur!" But then my school made this no-button rule for some reason. My mom and Claire's and some others are helping us appeal it on the grounds that it "inhibits our freedom of speech . . ." but that's another story. . . .

"Ooh!" I heard Ruby squeal behind me as she opened her own locker. "Look what I got! A little bear! Look! It says 'Merry Christmas.' How cute!"

I turned and glared straight at her.

"C'mon," Claire said, gently turning me around. "Let's go talk to Mrs. Bailey now, before the bell rings."

I sighed and nodded, but then just as I closed my locker I suddenly stopped.

Nick was coming.

He was running, still with his coat on, but he flashed us a quick look (not a smile exactly; more of a straight-on stare) as he went by. I was too slow, of course (as always), to even think of saying "Hi."

Instead, I watched him jog up to his locker and drop his bag. Claire started to walk away, but I grabbed her sleeve and held her back. We weren't going anywhere yet. I wanted to see Nick open his locker and find what Claire had left . . . though from the way he kept looking over his shoulder at us, I realized a more casual approach than just standing and staring was in order.

So I turned to my miserable locker and opened it once again. Then I pulled Claire behind the open door and *casually* peered around the side.

He opened his locker slowly and seemed to take a minute to sigh. He pulled out the Colts pad and pen and pencil that Claire had tied together, then put them back, hung up his coat, tossed in his hat, pulled out a notebook, and closed the door.

Then he headed off toward English, leaving Claire looking puzzled and me feeling even worse than before.

Claire looked at me. "I thought he liked the Colts."

My shoulders felt heavy. "So did I?" My whole body, in fact, felt heavy, from my head to my somewhat numb feet. I thought I *knew* Nick. I thought he'd *like* that stuff. I thought that even though we didn't talk as much as we used to, we were still, technically, friends. But it looked like somewhere along the way this fall, he'd *really* drifted away. I'd always thought that Nick and I were . . . well, that we were meant to be, and that one day he'd realize it, too, and we'd live happily ever after. But all of a sudden, as I stood there I realized there was a chance I could be . . . wrong.

"I'm sorry," I told Claire. "Can I tell you how much I hate this day?"

And it didn't get any better in homeroom either, where Claire and I arrived too late to say anything about my deadbeat Secret Santa to Mrs. Bailey.

She seemed, however, to maybe know something was up, the way she started the class by asking us all how Secret Santa was going.

"Great!" said Ruby. "This is the best thing we've ever done!" She shook her head back and forth, I know to show off her mistletoe earrings . . . the same earrings I remembered seeing in the cart she and Tallulah were sharing the weekend before. . . . And to think that she was going to tell Mrs. Bailey on Claire and me if *we* traded? I mean, I didn't have any proof, but really! What were the odds that *that* happened by chance? I mean, you tell me!

"I'm glad," said Mrs. Bailey. "But just remember, class" — she looked at Ruby — "I want this to be fun for you — you guys have certainly earned it this year — but I also want you to take advantage of this opportunity to think about your classmates and show them that you care."

(I won't even get into the comments and snickers that followed here. I mean, I'm sure you can imagine.)

"Quiet, please. As I was saying . . . I know I wasn't here last Friday, but I'm hoping a lot of you drew the name of someone you don't know that well, and that over the course of the week you'll take the time to get to know them better. And I think you'll find — or at least I hope you will — that the more thoughtful the gift you give someone, no matter how small, the more it will mean to both of you. It's easy to come to these holidays," she went on, "thinking just about what we can *get*. But let's see what it's like to really think about what we can give, *hmm,* shall we?"

I turned to glance at Mia, to see how she'd react to this. *Did she look guilty?* I wondered. Had Mrs. Bailey's speech about *giving* shamed her into tears? But no . . . she looked pretty normal, really. Sullen and aloof and completely annoying, as always.

"Oh, and it's unfortunate, but since we're not magical beings like the *real* Santa Claus, I know that once in a while there can be *little* problems with the system. All I can say is, please don't worry. These things always get straightened out. And if you do have any problems, please come to me so I can help you. I'm happy to. It's my job! Okay. Thanks, guys. . . . Now, who here has read — and I mean read, not seen the movie — Charles Dickens's *A Christmas Carol?*"

I turned to Claire and set my arms, crossed, on the top of my desk. We'd *definitely* say something to Mrs. Bailey after class.

"Um . . . Mrs. Bailey . . ."

She was standing by the blackboard, erasing the list we'd made that morning comparing and contrasting the three ghosts who visit Scrooge. She was wearing another Christmas sweater, different than the one she'd worn on Monday. This one, I noticed now that I was closer, featured the gifts from the "Twelve Days of Christmas" song. I think I liked Monday's snowman theme better — but I'm not sure.

Anyway, she turned around and let her glasses drop down over her seven swans, brushed back the one pure white lock in her otherwise black hair, and warmly smiled at us.

"Yes, Noel? Yes, Claire? What can I do for you?"

I took a breath . . . and swallowed. "It's my Secret Santa," I said. "I think I have one of those little problems you were talking about. . . ."

"Yes." Mrs. Bailey nodded. "I think I know about that."

I'm sure my mouth fell open and I looked like a total fool. "You do?"

71

"Yes." She kept nodding in that slow way that all teachers and, I think, most doctors have. "I think so. And I'm sure it's been very frustrating."

I frowned. "*Very*. And I don't think it's very fair. I mean, I don't know. . . . Are you going to fail her?"

Mrs. Bailey's eyebrows jumped. Then they bunched up as she clasped her hands.

"Ah . . . no," she said simply. Her lips worked from side to side. "In fact" — she let out a sigh — "I think it's going to be fine now."

She looked kind of thoughtful, then turned to her desk and pulled two candy canes out of a red and white glass jar. "Want one?" she asked.

Claire and I took them and thanked her.

"I think your Secret Santa will come through today, Noel," Mrs. Bailey said gently. "And I *know* they're very sorry for keeping you waiting. *Extremely* so. Of course, let me know right away if there's still a problem, though, won't you?"

I nodded. "Okay, Mrs. Bailey."

She smiled a smile that made me feel better, but somehow at the same time made me feel a little small, also. "I trust your own giving's going smoothly. . . ?" she asked me.

I cut my eyes to Claire. "Oh yeah. No problem there," I answered.

"Good. That's so important, too, isn't it?"

"Uh-huh."

"I'll see you two tomorrow, then?"

"Uh-huh," I said again. And with a wave and a "Thanks. See ya later," the two of us left.

"I wonder how she knew?" I said to myself as well as Claire.

We were walking down the hall, both working carefully to unwrap our candy canes without them breaking.

"Maybe Mia went to her already," suggested Claire. "Maybe she asked again if she could get out of it," she said.

"Hmm . . ." I nodded and slipped the long end of the candy cane into my mouth. It tasted minty and cool (of course), and I had to fight with my teeth not to crunch it all up right then.

"I wonder . . ." I said.

I wondered if Mia had already talked to Mrs. Bailey . . . and if she had, I wondered what she'd said. I also wondered if she'd *really* try harder now to be a good Santa . . . or if she'd do it but be totally lame. I mean, I had to figure . . .

I rolled the sweet stick around on my tongue, then let out the most cynical "Ha!" ever.

"What?" said Claire.

"You would not believe," I said, "what *I* left in *her* locker today."

"What?" asked Claire.

I pulled out my candy cane. "Think *everything*!" I said. Then I popped it back in.

Claire looked at me a little cockeyed. "Why?" she said.

"I don't know. . . ." I shrugged a little — kind of knowing whatever I said wasn't going to sound right.

Then we reached our lockers and split up to get our other books. The halls were clearing and we knew the bell for second period would be ringing soon.

I dialed my combination and with a yank pulled open the door — just as Claire called, "Hey! Looks like my Secret Santa's been here."

"Guess what," I said, staring into my locker. "Mine too."

CHAPTER SEVEN

It wasn't much. But it was something. Specifically: a bag of holiday peanut M&M's, a pair of polyester Santa socks (one size fits all), and a quickly written note on a piece of notebook paper.

Dear Noel,

I am so sorry. I left your locker combination in the North Pole (Ho-ho-ho!) on Monday and couldn't leave you anything until today.

I hope you like them.

Sincerely,

Your Secret Santa

Well, I thought, as I stowed my candy cane in my mouth and held the socks up for inspection, thanks to this project, I did know a few more things about Mia: She had much messier handwriting than I ever would have guessed, and she knew absolutely nothing about *me!*

"So?" Claire said eagerly, coming up behind me. "What'd you get? Let me see! And, hey, look at me!"

I turned to see Claire modeling a fuzzy purple scarf — almost exactly like the kind *I* was planning to make her. I couldn't believe it! And, I've got to say, neither could she.

Still sucking on her own candy cane, she tossed one end over her shoulder and grinned like crazy at me. "I *love* it!" she said. "But I don't get it. Did my Secret Santa get you to make it for me?" She took the other end of the scarf and wagged it teasingly at me. "You are so totally sneaky! Who is it? You've gotta tell me!"

I think my face was pretty much stuck in a combined look of intense irritation and total surprise, and it took me a second to pull out my candy cane and answer her. . . .

"I don't know."

"So you didn't make this?" she said. She was now holding both hairy ends and offering them up before me.

I shook my head. "No."

She laid the scarf down over her sweater and rubbed it thoughtfully with her hands.

"Really," she said. "Oh . . ."

I stared back at her.

"Weird. Well, maybe they bought it," she said, shrugging. "It is really well made. So what did your Secret Santa finally leave *you*?"

Still annoyed, I held up the socks and, I'm sure, rolled my eyes.

"Oh, they're cute!" said Claire.

"Well, you can have them," I told her.

"Why?"

I clicked my tongue and let my mouth fall, disappointed to the extreme. "Because I don't wear socks. Remember?" I held out my foot and pulled up my jeans to help remind her. "I haven't worn them all year."

"Oh, right." Claire nodded. "Well . . . maybe I will take them. They are cute."

"Here," I said, handing them over. "And you can have these, too." I took the M&M's out of my locker and offered them to her, too. "I'd rather have plain."

"Oh, come on," she said. She took the socks, but carefully put back the candy.

"I would," I swore. "I like them better. And

besides . . ." I picked up the heavy green bag to examine it further. ". . . it's probably re-gifted." I sneered.

"You think?" said Claire.

"Oh, I know. It's *exactly* like the bag I left in Mia's locker — the one that was still there this morning when I looked."

Claire's forehead wrinkled enough to move her bangs. "So?" she said. "They all look the same." She even laughed. (I'm so not kidding! Let's just say I was peeved.) "And," she went on, "you don't know for *sure* that it's Mia. I thought you liked peanut okay. You can always take them to lunch and trade."

I stared back at her in her fluffy new scarf (so *now* what was I going to get her?!) and her *conveniently* matching lavender sweater, holding my admittedly cute, if completely *inappropriate* Santa socks, and . . . well, I'm not proud, I'll admit it, but I completely flipped out.

"You know, it's really easy for you to look on the bright side," I snapped. "You have a Secret Santa with awesome taste and at least a clue. And I won't even get *into* whose Secret Santa you get to *be*." I glared. "I have somebody for both things who doesn't care at all! And it's really . . ." The word "unfair" was drowned out, unfortunately, by the second-period bell. "And now we're going to be late for French," I spat. "That's just great."

I slammed my locker, completely forgetting to get my French book, and had to dial my combination again six or seven times to get it back open. Claire, to her credit, stood by patiently and waited, breathing rather noisily, but not saying a word.

We got to French just as Mia was walking around, passing out a handout, and when she looked at me I'm not sure who was the first to look away. (Come to think of it, maybe she was.)

"*Bonjour, mesdemoiselles,*" said Madame Greenwood, perky as always, from the front of the room. "*Mais pourquoi êtes-vous en retard pour classe, mes amies?*"

Huh? is right. Was she asking if we were late, maybe? I bit my lip and turned to Claire.

"*Je ne sais pas . . . ?*" she said with a shrug.

Good old "I don't know." I should have tried that. It always works.

"Ah . . . *naturellement.*" The teacher nodded and with a sigh and a sweep of her arm, ushered us to our waiting *chaises*. (That word I know.) "*Mais, s'il vous plaît,*" she went on, "*jetez les* candy canes." She pointed to the green metal trash can and though I don't know what she was actually *saying,* I think she made herself pretty clear.

Too bad, I thought, as I let my candy cane fall in with a startlingly loud clank. (Claire's followed right away.) I had almost gotten it down to a needle-sharp point. What a waste, but typical, I guessed, for such a bummer of a day.

I slipped into my chair and kept my head down as Mia continued with her rounds, but when she finally got to me I couldn't help but look at her again. I guess I wanted her to see, in my eyes, that I had gotten her *barely* sorry note and her so-called gifts . . . and I was also kind of curious to see if she'd gotten mine. I wanted to see if she was wearing the holiday earrings I had given her or the lip gloss. . . . But no. No earrings. Lips dull. She was determined to ruin this whole Secret Santa thing, wasn't she, I thought. Or maybe not the *whole* thing, I realized. Really, she was just ruining mine!

Well, two could play that game.

As she put down the handout, I pulled up my foot and set it right down, blatantly *sockless,* on the top of my desk. I crossed my arms and made my lips tight and straight not to be messed with, as I looked her in the face.

She looked back at me with these wide eyes that I just knew were saying *"Touché!"*

"Noel! Retires ton pied! Immediatement!"

Madame Greenwood's voice, still powerful for a such a tiny woman — especially one who's even older than my grandmother, I'm sure — blasted at me from across the room.

Oops. I got the distinct impression the words she'd said meant "get your feet down!" so I instantly sat up and tried to look busy. But, seriously, if you think I concentrated for one second on that worksheet . . . well, let's just say you should really think again.

In fact, I think it's safe to say that just about the *only* thing I concentrated on at all that day was how utterly miserable my life was. Oh, I guess I'm exaggerating . . . a little. Just the whole holiday part of it, that's all.

Science was a complete blur. But at least I didn't have to do a lab.

Lunch was complete torture. Everyone, and I do mean everyone, was not just going *on,* but on and on and *on,* about their oh-so-very amazing, most stupendously awesome Secret Santas.

"Did you see my bracelet? I am *so* wearing it in Cancún!"

"Isn't this photo book *too* cute! I can totally put all my pictures from Costa Rica in it!"

"Wait! Did you get those Santa tights? No way! Me too! They'll be so cute under my ski pants!"

Ruby and Tallulah, as I'm sure you can imagine, were among the very worst — and the *first*, I might add, to ask me what *I* had to show.

"I got some socks," I said.

"Cute! Can we see?"

"No."

And while I have to admit Claire was nice enough not to bring up her scarf too much . . . she was still *wearing* it, which meant everyone *saw* it, and so couldn't help *notice* that it was supercute.

"Ooh! I love your scarf so much! I want one, too. Where'd you get it?"

"Uh . . . from my Secret Santa."

"No way! Do you think they made it?"

"I don't know."

"Hey! Noel knits!" said Olivia.

"Do you think it's her?" Isabelle asked Claire.

She shook her head. "Mm, I don't think so."

"No?" Olivia looked doubtful . . . and even stopped by me on her way back from the salad bar later on. "Are you?" she asked, whispering.

"Am I what?" I said.

"Claire's Secret Santa. Hmm? I promise I won't tell."

"I could tell you," I said drearily, "but I'd have to kill you then, you know."

Meanwhile, down at the other end of the table, the boys were comparing baseball cards and comic books and whatever else they collect. Cole was passing out *more* Hershey Kisses to the jeers and shouts of "Cole, I think someone *loves* you" from most everyone. And Nick was letting them all take turns with his Santa hat and Rudolph nose. When the hat got back to him he put it on and shyly smiled, and for a second all I could think about was how nice and cute he was . . . how easy it was to like him . . . and how brave he was to put a hat on his head that had just been worn by Colin. . . . *Eww.*

But then, *of course,* he caught me staring at him (as he *always* does, like I said), and everything that had been bumming me out all day came flooding back — with interest, as my dad would say.

I did do as Claire suggested and brought my candy down to lunch, and I made some decent trades. But nothing — not even half of Abby's cupcake — tasted as good as it should have.

Honestly, I was tempted to go off and sit by myself. But the only empty chairs were at the table Mia was sitting at — plotting, like some super-villain, some new scheme for the ultimate destruction of Secret Santa for me, I was sure. So I just sat there and tried to choke down my M&M's and bite-size Milky Ways and Texas-style school barbecue instead.

Before fifth period, I almost, *almost* went back to Mrs. Bailey, I have to admit. But when I thought about it, I didn't know what I'd say. I mean, my Secret Santa had left *something*... and a half-decent note of explanation for the day before. Honestly, when I tried to find the *words* to explain what was so wrong with Mia, I couldn't seem to. But I sure could *feel* it!

The day went on, basically without me. I stumbled through gym (even though we were jump roping, and I normally *love* that), and I made my way through world history without saying a word — not even to Nick, which was a shame, since for once he actually spoke to *me*.

"Can I borrow your eraser for a second?" he said.

And all I could do, I swear, was hand it over and stare.

"Uh . . . thanks," he said when he had finished.

I think I nodded, but you know what? I'm not even sure.

By the time math rolled around, I so totally and completely wanted to go home, I could hardly see straight. The end-of-day bell rang and I grabbed my stuff and practically ran through the halls to get my coat from my locker and go.

"Hey, Speedy," said Claire. "What's the hurry?"

I didn't even turn. I kept facing my *incredibly* plain locker and devoted myself entirely to getting my combination right on the first try.

Yes! I thought at first. Then, *Oh no . . . not again!*

"Well?" Claire said.

"I'm just done with this day," I sort of mumbled. "I wanna get out of here, that's all."

"Do you want to come to *my* house?" she asked. "My sister made cookies yesterday."

"Really?" I said.

"Yeah, a *lot*! I mean, most of them were for her boyfriend, but she left a few for us."

Hmm . . . I opened my locker and picked through its *very* plain insides for what I would need that night at home. I was kind of sick of sweets, to be honest, but going home with Claire was always fun.

85

I was just about to say "Yeah, okay, why not," when Claire just *had* to go on. . . .

"And, I don't know, it's only Tuesday, but I feel like I need more stuff for Nick. . . . I was thinking a friendship bracelet for later in the week? And you're so good at making them, could you help me?"

I grabbed my coat, my *least* favorite hat (I seemed to have lost all my others already), and my *most* favorite pink and gray striped scarf, then at last I turned around.

"A friendship bracelet?" I said. "You want *me* to help *you* make a friendship bracelet for the guy *I* like? Are you kidding? Isn't it enough that I already helped you pick out everything else for him? I mean, really! And, come to think of it," (I was on a roll now) "isn't it enough that you clearly have an absolutely awesome Secret Santa who can provide you with all the scarves — and who knows what else — you'll ever need? Maybe you should get *them* to help you."

I could feel my eyes burning and my throat getting tight and totally sore, and it was all I could do to keep standing there with her looking at me all shocked and hurt and wounded and . . . well, like *you* would have looked at me, too, I'm sure.

But I wasn't done yet. Oh no.

"So, no, Claire," I went on, "I *don't* want to go to your house this afternoon. Thanks. And you know what . . . ?" With inspiration that could only have come from deep despair, I reached into my most uncool black backpack and pulled out her invitation. ". . . I don't even think I want to go your party Friday night either." I handed it back to her with a gulp. "Thanks, anyway. Good-bye."

And with that, I stormed out the door into the cold.

I know. *I know.* I was the biggest jerk in the whole world. Believe me, I know!

But I didn't look back. No way. I kept going. Eyes straight ahead and *almost* but not quite overflowing with tears, down the line of chugging buses, toward the one that would deliver me from this den of misery and unjustness otherwise known as school.

Then some idiot hit me in the head with a football . . . and I couldn't help it, I totally cried.

❄ CHAPTER EIGHT ❄

By the time I got home from school that day, I swear it was getting dark, and half the holiday lights on my street had already been turned on. Now, normally I love that stuff. The more icicle lights dripping from your roof and inflatable snow globes in your yard, I say, the better. But as you can probably guess, I wasn't quite feeling the holiday spirit that afternoon. No, in fact all I could think as I trudged up my driveway, my lashes still damp and practically frozen, was how totally lame my neighbors' houses made my own look.

I mean, it was almost exactly one week till Christmas and we hadn't even put electric candles in our windows yet. We always did that. Come on! And there were still no lights on the balsam fir in our yard either — the one that had started out as our live Christmas tree the Christmas after Cecee was born. My dad had blanketed it with more and more colored lights every year since then . . . until now.

So, what? I thought. Did having a new baby mean you didn't think about Christmas anymore? Did it mean, I wondered, that in addition to being blown off by Santa at school, I could look forward to being blown off by him at home, as well? I mean, I seriously doubted that my mom had made any time for Christmas shopping between all her doctors' appointments and compulsive "nesting" and napping. (Not that I had done much either, but I'd been planning to the next weekend, I swear.)

Anyway, I got to my door — the *one* part of my house that had been decked, you might say (with a wreath from the grocery store) — and opened it to find a house I didn't recognize at all.

"Mom! What's going on here?" I called.

"Hang on. I'm coming. . . ."

Now, first of all, let me explain how my house *normally* looks: I guess you could call it — oh, I don't know — something like "comfortably messy." We're not slobs or anything, trust me, but we're not exactly obsessive about cleaning things up either. (Not like Claire's house — thank goodness! — where her dad is *always* vacuuming and reminding you to take your shoes off.) There's always some kind of pile of something at the bottom of the stairs, and a month's worth of mail covering the dining room table, *but* there's always a clean glass (when you want one) and clean underwear (if you look), plus — and this is the best part — you can be sure that when you put something down, no one else is going to pick it up!

Now let me describe how it looked that day when I got home: just like Claire's house! I mean, right down to the vacuum tracks on the rugs!

My mom waddled in from the kitchen, beaming.

"Hi, hon! How was school?"

"Mom!" I said, practically screaming. "What have you done?"

She looked around and took a deep breath of lemony-fresh air. "I know," she sighed. "Isn't it nice?"

"No!" I barked. "It's not!" I looked around the foyer. "Where's my iPod? Where are my shoes? Where are the library books I keep forgetting to take to school?"

I think my mom was about to answer, but I was already off to the next room.

"Where's my address book?" I shouted. "Where's my knitting? Where's my brush? I left it right here on the table. And all my pins! It's half my collection! Where'd they go?"

I turned to find my mom behind me, her arms crossed, resting on her stomach, staring at me like she does at that kid who rides his bike across our lawn.

"It's all up in your room."

"Oh." Then I panicked. "You didn't!"

"Don't worry," she said. "I didn't touch your room." She made a face. "Egh." Then she grinned.

She used the hem of her tent of a shirt to rub a fingerprint smudge off the table, and said, "Let me know if you can't find anything." Then she looked at me harder. "Hey, honey, is something else wrong? Did something happen at school?"

Determined not to cry again, I stared up at the ceiling (it looked the same, at least) and swallowed.

"Hmm?" she asked.

"No," I said.

"You sure?" she asked.

"Yes," I told her. Then I started to turn to go.

"Hey. Want to clean the pantry with me? I could really use your help."

I shook my head. "No, Mom, I don't." (Was she, like, for real?) "I just want to be alone."

"Okay." She sounded satisfied. "But first, give me a hug."

I know it probably sounds awful, but I'm pretty sure I groaned.

"Oh, come on," she said.

"But it's *hard* to hug you, Mom."

Now, don't get me wrong. I *like* to hug my mom as much as the next girl, of course. But I wasn't kidding. Lately it was not an easy job.

I don't remember having as much trouble before Cecee was born. But maybe it's because I was so much smaller. Now when I hugged my mom it felt like we had an exercise ball between us. There was nowhere for my arms to go, or my head. . . . Plus I had this idea in my mind that somehow, I don't know, I might hurt . . . it.

Still, I did my best, and my mom kissed my cheek and *finally* let me escape to my room.

"Be ready for dinner when Dad gets home," she called. "He's bringing Indian."

"Again?" I had to stop and turn around. We'd just had it, what, on Sunday?

She grinned as she rubbed her stomach. "What can I say?" she said.

I climbed the stairs and stopped in the bathroom as I made a silent wish: *Would the aliens that stole my life, please be so kind as to return it?* It had all been going so perfectly fine and average till then.

Then I looked down to see my fly was open and realized, to my horror, it had probably been like that all day at school. . . .

I knew I should have worked on my history paper that afternoon, and probably studied French, too, but after making it through my math homework, I just couldn't focus anymore. I needed to take my mind off school, which meant there was really only one thing to do: listen to my favorite sad-song playlist (courtesy, via Claire, of her sister) and re-reread my most current favorite book.

Besides, I wanted to enjoy the privacy of my room while I still had it, even if it did look more like a little kid's room than a teenager's. (Okay, *almost* teenager.) Not that anyone had said any-thing *directly* about Cecee moving from her room into mine — the plan right now was for the new baby to stay in my parents' room — but I was no fool. I knew the day would come when the baby needed a room of its own. . . .

Of course, finding my music in the giant basket of stuff my mother had dumped on my bed wasn't easy, nor was finding my book. Don't ask me how books I've read hundreds of times find their way to the back of my closet, while clothes I never wear end up dangling from my bookshelves. I honestly couldn't tell you. All I know is somehow they do.

A couple of hours later, there was a knock at my door.

(Of course, I couldn't hear it with my headphones on.)

Then the door swung open and Cecee stood there, frowning, wearing black jeans, a black skull-covered T-shirt, and a much longer blue veil than I'd ever seen before.

"Dinnertime!" she screamed.

I put down my book.

"I bet you can't guess what!"

"Indian," I said.

Her eyes got big — like two samosas. "You're right! How'd you know?"

"Just psychic," I told her. Then I waved her away. "Now, go," I told her. "I'll be down in just a sec."

"Hurry," she warned me. "Oh, and Claire called," she added, "while I was on the phone. I forgot to tell you." (I refrained from a sarcastic "thanks.") "But Mom said to tell you to call her back after dinner."

This time the "thanks" came out, sarcasm and all.

You know, things like that just don't happen to people who have their own phones. . . .

"I don't know, Colleen . . ." my dad was saying as I walked into the kitchen, "the way you're working around this place, I say that baby's getting ready to come pretty soon."

"Oh please!" said my mom. "Don't even say things like that, Paul!"

Yeah, I thought, *Dad, please!*

My mom wrapped her hands around her stomach. "I *need* another month!"

At least, I thought.

"Hello, sunshine," said my dad, when he finally noticed me. "How are you doing?"

"Fine, I guess." I sighed and made some sort of bored and irritated face. "Can we just eat?"

"Dig in," said my mom. "Oh, but hang on there, missy." She was looking at Cecee. "No headdresses at the table . . . and I'm not sure I want you wearing the baby's new blanket either. . . ."

Ah, that was it, I realized. Cecee had switched her old pillowcase for the fancy blue blanket Grandma Janice had just sent. Wishful thinking on her part, of course. I so totally knew the baby was going to be a girl.

"But Mom," Cecee whined, "I'm going to be Mary. *Mary.* I can't wear a *pillowcase.* This blanket is perfect. *Please?* Come on!"

"'Come on'?" said my mom. She let out a kind of snort and shared that look she likes to share with my dad. "We'll talk about it later. Right now, just take it off."

Cecee did as she was told, with a face that looked a lot like one of mine, then we passed around the breads and rice and spicy chicken we seemed to never have enough of, along with the weird-looking vegetable side dishes no one ever seemed to touch.

Of all the things my mom could crave, it could have been a lot worse, I decided.

"Hey, Noel," my mom spoke up, "I was thinking tomorrow, when I go to the store, I could get some stuff for making a gingerbread house, like the one you made last year."

If I remember correctly, I didn't say much.

"It might be fun," she went on. "And you could get Cecee to help you."

"Yeah!" shouted Cecee.

They all looked at me, I know, expecting some holly-jolly-hallelujah-it's-Christmas, yessirree!

But what is the point? I was thinking. Christmas, I'd decided, just wasn't going to be Christmas this year . . . at all. Why pretend it would be?

I didn't *say* this, of course.

What I did say was this: "You know what? I don't know why I should bother decorating some stupid cookie house for you when no one has bothered at all to decorate our real one. You know what our neighbors are thinking, don't you? They're thinking we're a bunch of losers. And you know what? We are. I'm done." I went and stood up. "Good night."

I'm not exactly sure what came over me. I just couldn't help it, that's all I can say. That, and that the rest of my night was pretty much ruined.

Of course, my mom came up later to — let's face it — lecture me.

"You know, Noel," she said, "you can be mad, that's fine. And sad, of course. And I'm sorry. But it's not okay to be mean to Cecee or Dad or me."

I looked past her head, at the pink ballet shoe border along the top edge of my wall.

"And your point is?" I said.

"My point is," she said sternly, "that I know Claire's having a party on Friday, and if you keep acting this way, you will not be going."

That's when I looked at her.

"Fine," I said.

I know . . . I can be an idiot.

So, of course I couldn't leave my room for the rest of the night. Not when my mom asked if I was still hungry . . . and if I had anything to *say*. Not when my dad asked if I wanted to play a few hands of cards . . . and if I had anything to *say*. Not even when Cecee knocked and asked if I wanted to watch the Peanuts Christmas special on TV.

"It's so babyish," she said. "But it's on and I know it's your favorite."

"Thanks, but no," I told her.

"Oh, and Mom and Dad wondered if you had anything to *say*."

I didn't even come out when I realized I still hadn't called Claire back. She'd really think I was mad at her, I knew. But it was probably best. Clearly, I wasn't responsible for the things I was saying to people that day. Not that I was looking forward to the next day, exactly, but I sure couldn't wait for this one to be over with already. . . .

✻ CHAPTER NINE ✻

So Wednesday came, of course, as I knew it would, and after a round of "Are you feeling better" and "We love you, Noel, you know" — plus an "I love you, too; I'm really sorry," from me — I set off for school.

I got there fully knowing (and not feeling too bad about it either) that I didn't have a single thing to leave in Mia's locker — and I felt even less bad when I opened up my own.

There was *another* pair of socks. I swear. No jokes.

This pair was neon green with hotpink candy canes all over — and while I thought they were kind of awesome, they really bummed me out.

I don't wear socks! I wanted to scream out.

I never have (this *school year, at least), and I never will!*

I'm sure I was growling or sputtering or something as I fished out my textbooks and slammed the door — which is probably why Claire looked at me funny from behind her own locker door.

I knew I should say something . . . I even opened my mouth. But nothing came out — not before Claire pulled out a handful of fuzzy purple wool and pulled it down around her head. It was a hat to match yesterday's scarf. I could have puked it was so cute.

"Ooh!" cried Olivia, running up behind us. "Claire! Ooh! Look at you! From your Secret Santa?"

She nodded. "Mm-hmm."

"You lucky duck!" said Olivia. "Oh, but look what I got today!" She held out a sheet of tiny, teardrop-shaped jewels in a rainbow of gold-trimmed colors. One, I could see, was missing . . . and, when I looked up, I saw it on Olivia's forehead, between her eyes.

"A whole pack of bindis!" she went on. "From *India*! I can wear them when I do *yoga*! In Cancún! Aren't they cool? Want one?" she said, turning to offer the sheet to me.

I shook my head. "No thanks." And pulled my books close to my chest.

She shrugged. "It wards off bad luck."

I *should* have taken one, I thought. But it was too late. I so hate it when I do that.

"You?" she said to Claire.

"Yeah, sure," said Claire. "Why not?"

Claire took a purple one — to match her hat and scarf, I guess — but I turned and walked away even before she put it on.

It's not that I wasn't talking to Claire, you know. It wasn't like that at all. It was more like I *couldn't* talk to her, couldn't bring myself to say "I'm sorry about yesterday and all." Which, I guess, in a way, was almost as bad. Yeah, I know.

Anyway, I went on to homeroom, bracing myself for the Parade of What I Got Today that had probably already begun. But when I got there, the room was half empty. I knew all those kids weren't still at their lockers. . . . *What's going on?* I wondered.

Not that Ruby and Tallulah, and the kids that were there, weren't doing their part.

"Smell me," said Melanie, offering me her arm. "Guess what it is. Go on."

"Oatmeal?" I said dully, very much not wanting to play along.

"No!" she said. She frowned and pulled it away. "Gingerbread cookies, of course!"

"Oh."

"My Secret Santa sent me a new ringtone for my phone!" said Ruby. She played it back for us. *Jingle bell, jingle bell, jingle bell rock . . .* "How*ever* did he know my number, do you think?" she gushed.

I looked at Tallulah. Yeah, I wondered . . . *not!*

"What are those?" Melanie asked Isabelle.

"Oh, they're these postcards I got today," she said. "Aren't they too cute? Here, take one."

Isabelle handed one to each kid around her, including Olivia and Claire, who'd just come in all bindied up and happy to share.

While everyone *ooh*ed and *ahh*ed and picked out their own jewels, I focused on my postcard, with its cute picture of a real penguin chick with a cartoon scarf added on, and wondered why *I* couldn't have gotten some of those.

"Write your address on it," Isabelle told me and everybody else, "and I can write to you from Vail!"

Great, I thought. *That's just what I needed over my vacation: to be reminded* again *of how sad and lame it was.*

Still, I wrote down my name and address . . . and shot a bitter look over to Mia as I did.

With so many seats empty, she looked even

more out of it and alone, and I could tell (I mean, it was obvious!) she thought whatever we were doing over on our side of the room was *inane*. I caught her eye and we stared at each other for a second, then she looked down at her desk and let her hair form its usual shield.

I wondered what she'd been looking forward to most on her way to school that morning: finding yet more awesome stuff to ignore (or worse, laugh at) in her locker; or leaving more stuff she knew I'd hate in mine.

Well, I suddenly thought to myself, I was glad I hadn't given her the satisfaction of the first thing; why should I let her enjoy the second one either?

I also snuck a look at Nick, who was inspecting Cole's license plate magnet, and I guess I wanted him to think I was super-happy and having a wonderful time, too.

So I sat up straighter and tried to look less like a girl for whom life had no meaning and more like someone having a *ridiculous* amount of fun.

"These are too cute, Isabelle!" I declared (I think rather loudly) as I handed back her postcard. "Make sure you write to me *first* next week, okay!"

"Oh, I totally will," she assured me, "since I know you're going to be home."

Yeah, I know. But I just swallowed and kept smiling.

"Good morning, class," said Mrs. Bailey, since I guess the bell had just rung. Her sweater that day had all nine of Santa's reindeer eagerly pulling his sleigh, and as she waved to us their gold-ribbon bridles jingled. "I have to tell you class, how much I just love seeing all the thoughtful gifts you've picked out for one another, and I can only imagine how good you all feel when you see how happy your friends are to receive them."

There were a lot of smiles and "Yeah"s and nods (though, of course, not from me and Mia).

"Keep up the good work," she went on. "I'd actually love to talk about how this project's going a little more with the whole class . . ."

Great, I thought.

". . . but I'm afraid right now we have to line up."

Oh, that's right, I remembered. *The holiday assembly was today. That's* where all the missing kids were — preparing to wow us with their dubious choral and woodwind and whatever else skills.

"If you did bring anything to class," announced Mrs. Bailey, "just leave it at your desk. There'll be time to collect it after the concert. Now, everyone behind Ruby, quickly please, students. And quietly."

As we all lined up, I attempted what had become my usual tactic in these situations, coolly positioning myself between Claire *and* Nick. Sometimes it worked, but sometimes it was hopeless and just too *obvious* to be cool, though Claire was always nice enough to help as best she could. Not this day, however. And it wasn't Nick who was hard to stand next to, it was Claire.

I guess by then she'd kind of decided that *she* wasn't talking to *me,* which did take a bit of the fun out of scoring a place next to Nick — that and the fact that I turned to find *Mia* on my other side, instead.

I breathed a deep but silent sigh as we joined the other lines of students already snaking through the halls.

Now, our school is kind of old — in fact, it used to be a high school — and it's full of lots of ancient stuff, like prehistoric science labs and bathrooms out, I swear, of the Dark Ages. But the auditorium is gorgeous. Claire says that when her sister went here, the seats were hard and gave you splinters. But somewhere, somehow, they got the money to fix it up and now we have blue-cushioned chairs, just like in a movie theater. Plus, some artist put up 3-D murals all around the room, and if you ever get tired of the program (particularly scholastic awards stuff and those quarterly addresses our principal, Mrs. Joseph, likes to give), you can always keep yourself entertained by just looking around.

So I really have to say that if you *do* manage to get a seat next to Nick Holiday, no matter what you have to sit through, the whole auditorium thing is pretty nice . . . usually.

Of course, as you've already guessed, I was not really in the mood. Not for holiday music courtesy of the chorus and, apparently, the jazz ensemble — and especially not for standing up at the end to sing along. (We all knew *that* was coming.) Not for angry looks from Claire, who was sitting down the row. Not for having to sit two inches from the Grinch of all Grinches herself (Mia, of course). And, to make it all even worse, I wasn't even in the mood to talk to Nick!

"So, uh . . ." he said, turning to me, "how's your Secret Santa?"

An innocent enough question . . . or so he thought, I'm sure!

I turned to him, thrilled to be noticed. But the question . . . boy, did it hit a raw nerve.

As the auditorium continued to fill around us, I looked down at my lap, all too conscious of the source of all my troubles to my right, and suddenly I realized what a fine opportunity I had: to both confide in my crush and *innocently* make my feelings about this whole Santa mess known. . . .

"Actually," I said as loudly as I thought I safely could, "my Secret Santa stinks."

"Huh?"

"Yeah." I nodded in what I thought was an appropriately pitiful way.

"Really? Why?" he asked.

(He *is* nice, isn't he?)

"Well," I sighed, "I mean, I thought the whole point was to try to get to know your person better, you know? And, well . . ." I sighed again. ". . . I don't think my Santa cares about getting to know me at all." I snuck a sidelong glance at Mia, just to see if she was listening. She had her golden shield around her, but I was pretty sure she was.

"Oh . . . well, what did they give you?"

Very sadly, I shook my head. "Socks."

"Oh," he said. "What? Don't you like . . . socks?"

"I mean, they're okay," I said, "but come on." I leaned back and set my Vans on the back of the seat in front of me, exposing my naked, still chilly and somewhat blue ankles, and causing the eighth grader in front of me to turn around and glare at me.

I put my feet down.

I looked at Nick like *"Can you believe it?,"* and I have to say, he did look concerned. *Maybe he does like me!* I thought.

Then he said, "What?"

"Socks," I said. "I so don't wear them. You know that, right?"

"I guess I did. . . ." he said, and he kind of smiled. (Kind-of smiles are the cutest, you know.) "But maybe your Secret Santa thought you needed them . . . or something. I don't know."

"Maybe," I said, really appreciating the effort. "But frankly," I said, raising my voice a decibel or two, "and, I mean, it's not like I care *at all* — don't you think that's almost *worse*?"

He thought it over for a second. Then he frowned. (This look's a pretty cute one, too, by the way.) "Are you sure that's all you got?"

"Yeah, basically," I said. I snuck another peek at Mia. "But don't get me wrong. It's no big deal. I still have my real friends, after all."

I sighed and smiled at him bravely.

In a movie, I thought, *this is when he'd take my hand.*

"Shhh."

Then Mrs. Bailey jingled past us, and the Dreidel Song began. . . .

An hour later, when the concert was over (and no, Nick still hadn't held my hand), Mrs. Bailey ushered us out with instructions to follow her back to her room if we needed to, or to go ahead to second period.

Nick was going back, I saw, and I was really, really torn. I felt like we'd finally *connected* after barely talking for so long, and I so wanted to walk back to homeroom with him . . . but I didn't want to seem too obvious.

Nick would have to wait, I finally decided. Maybe I could sit next to him at lunch . . . ! (Claire, it seemed, would not miss me.)

So I stopped in the bathroom, brushed my hair, and checked to make sure those odd looks from Nick had in fact been ones of pity, and not the eww-there's-something-stuck-in-your-teeth kind. *Please, no,* I thought. *Phew.* (They looked okay.)

Then I hurried down the hall to the stairs back up to the second floor.

But then I stopped — because there was Mia, standing by her open locker, *crying.* I mean, she didn't even seem to care that all these sixth graders were watching. She was just letting the tears *go.*

Wow, I thought, *the things I said must have hit her* hard*!*

I mean, I'd wanted to her to feel guilty for letting me down like that, I know. But I'd honestly never meant to — or thought that I *could* even — make her *cry.* I'd thought she was made of stone. Mean, old, stuck-up, too-cool-to-bother-with-you stone. But right then she looked — would you believe it — even more upset than me.

Have I gotten her all wrong? I wondered as I stood there feeling kind of cold and mean and queasy. Had I made her feel like a total fool? Had she really *tried* to be a thoughtful Secret Santa to me? *Well, she sure hasn't tried very hard,* I thought.

But then again, I had to tell myself, neither had I.

I almost — *almost* — walked right up to her and told her I was sorry. Sorry for saying she was a bad Secret Santa. And sorry for being such a lousy one myself this morning.

But, well, that's harder than you think.

Instead I just kind of stood there while the sixth graders scampered away, and tried to think how I could creep by without her seeing me.

Then she turned, and I totally cringed, I think. But she wasn't looking at me. She was putting a photo back on the inside of her locker door, where it had come from. It was one of those pictures of those kids from her old school. . . .

And then, I guess, it struck me: Here I was with plenty of friends around (less than some, perhaps, but more than others, clearly) and I was pushing them away, and here Mia didn't have *any* because she'd had to leave them all.

And that's not all. I'd been so obsessed with her not getting to know *me* better, when I hadn't even tried to get to know her better at all. . . .

I mean, had I? I thought for a second. *Um . . . no. Definitely not.*

I was really kind of sorry. But still, I didn't go up and say so. She'd shut her locker and left by that time. And I was glad, I have to say.

It would be easier to show her, anyway. Or at least I hoped so.

You know, they say "misery loves company," but it's not entirely true. Even more than that, I think, misery wants to be happy, and to help make other people happy, too. At least I think I do.

✻CHAPTER TEN✻

By the time I got back to homeroom, second period had almost begun, and the room was filling with kids from Mrs. Bailey's next English class. I hurried to my desk and grabbed the books I'd left there, and stopped to give her a quick "hi" as I walked out.

"Noel, darling, I wanted to ask you," Mrs. Bailey stopped me with a smile, "if your Secret Santa problems had improved?"

I nodded and grinned and assured her, "It's going to be fine."

Then I sped through the halls to French, where I was *en retard*, once again. But it was okay for once, at least, because Madame Greenwood still wasn't there.

I glanced around, looking for Mia, but she didn't seem to be there either, so I plopped down in my usual seat behind Claire and hoped she'd turn around. She didn't, so after a minute I nudged her shoulder with my hand.

"Yes," she said stiffly, waiting a moment before turning around.

I leaned forward and said softly, "I'm really sorry. I really am."

"Well, you should be. *I* didn't do anything." She was frowning but I knew her well enough to know she was just as ready to make up as I was. "I even tried to call you last night."

"I know," I said. "Cecee told me . . . but then I got in this other fight at home . . . "

Her expression changed. "Really?"

"Oh, it's okay." I shrugged it off. "Just me being me again. But I'm okay today."

"Did your Secret Santa come?" She glanced at her scarf self-consciously, its fringy, purple fluff peeking out, here and there, from beneath her long brown hair, then looked back up with an expression of hopeful, best-friend concern.

"Well . . . yeah." I rolled my eyes a bit. "I got some more socks."

"You're kidding?" she said.

"Oh, no. I'm not."

"Hmm . . ." She turned around even more. "You know, maybe," she said, half-whispering, "Mia thinks you *need* socks. I don't know. Did you think of that?"

"Funny," I whispered back, "that's what Nick said."

Claire's expression changed again. "*Nick* said that? Really?" Of course, who knows what she was more amazed at: the fact that Nick had suggested the same thing, or that he'd simply talked to me at all.

"Mm-hmm," I said with a big smile, not trying to disguise my excitement one bit. "At assembly."

"Really?" she said again. "What else did he say?"

I kind of sighed and shrugged. "Not that much. But" — and I know I looked goofy here — "it was a nice start!"

"You know," Claire said, grinning, "that's something I was thinking, too."

"What?" I asked her.

"Maybe Nick acts so quiet around you because he likes you, too. . . ."

I shook my head. I *wished*. But no. "Not a chance," I said flatly. "I mean, you *know* when someone likes you."

"I guess." Claire shrugged.

"Anyway," I went on, "I think maybe I've been wrong about Mia. . . ." I leaned in closer and brought my voice down even lower. "I saw her crying after the assembly. By her locker."

"No way," said Claire. She glanced around quickly, trying to look for Mia, too. "Hey, where is she, do you think?"

"I don't know . . ."

"Why was she crying?"

"I'm not sure . . ." I said. I looked down at the floor, ashamed. "Maybe because she heard me complaining about her to Nick." I filled my lips with air so they made balloons around my teeth, then let it out with a guilty, wish-I-could-take-it-back, sorry hiss. "But I also think it's because she misses her old school," I went on. "And her old friends, you know." I looked at Claire. "I was even wondering if maybe you had another invitation. By the way, I am totally coming to your party." (Provided, of course, my mom said it was okay.) "What do you think?"

"Well, sure." Claire reached for her purse. "I mean, if you think so . . . why not?"

Just then, Madame Greenwood burst in, pushing a cart almost as big as her.

"*Bonjour, classe, voilà, la Bûche de Noël!* In other words," she said, smiling, "a yule log."

"I thought," she went on in English, "that since we only have class three times a week, and since we have a test on Friday," (she grinned; I groaned) "we should celebrate *Noël* today, *dans le français!*"

"Wow! Cool!" everyone said . . . except Ruby, who always has to say something like *"Ooh, la, la! C'est magnifique!"* (No kidding. True.)

And they (even Ruby) were right, because on the cart was a big silver tray with this chocolate-frosted cake that looked exactly like a log . . . right down to its nubby, cut-off, iced branches and light dusting of sugar snow. It even had little white — what was it, meringue? — mushrooms growing out of its creamy bark. Yum!

"C'est le gâteau traditionnel de Noël en France, mes chéris," said Madame Greenwood.

"Pardon?" said Josh.

"It's a traditional Christmas cake in France," she repeated slowly with a smile.

"Did you make it?" Tallulah asked.

"Mais oui!" she replied. "Of course, one you bought in a French bakery would be much more *détaillé,* as they say!"

116

"Can we . . . eat it?" asked Dustin.

"Ah . . ." Madame Greenwood nodded in her knowing, elflike way. *"Dans le français, s'il vous plaît."*

We all looked at each other, mouths watering but at the same time without any idea what to say.

The teacher sighed.

"Pouvons . . ." she said.

"Pouvons," we repeated.

"Nous . . ."

"Nous."

"Manger?"

"Manger."

"Mais oui! Et bon appetite!" She reached down and pulled out plates and forks and a wide knife from the cart's lower shelf and waved us toward her. "You know what that means, don't you?"

Colin shouted, "It means 'let's eat'!"

"Oui! Et Joyeux Noël!"

In case you didn't know, *that* means "Happy Noel." And I knew that if I could just make Mia a little happier, I really would be, too.

Those French might not know much about *le langage*, but they sure do have amazing desserts! Who knew that beneath all that chocolate icing bark would be this thin chocolate cake, all rolled

117

up like a spiral, around tons of totally delicious chocolate whipped cream? *Yum* is right!

Of course, I still wasn't looking forward to Friday's test any more, but it did make Wednesday's review a little easier to take.

And in case you were wondering, Mia got a piece of *bûche,* too, when she got to class near the end with a headache note from the nurse.

I was dying to put Claire's invitation in her locker after class, but my next class, earth science, was on the completely opposite end of the school. So I waited until after. Then, armed with the knowledge of how to tell sedimentary from metamorphic rocks (metamorphic rocks are layered and make a *ching* sound when you bang them; sedimentary rocks are usually light in color and weight; A-plus on that lab, thank you very much!), I delivered the silver envelope, with a note from me on the front.

This is basically what it said:

Dear Mia,

I'd like to get to know you better — but it's hard to do from the North Pole! Ho-ho-ho! But if you're free Friday night, maybe we can both get to know each other better, you know?

Yours truly,

S.S.

118

P.S. More presents to come tomorrow; forgot to pack my sleigh this morning. Ho-ho-ho!

I guess it wasn't exactly Shakespeare. But it's not always easy to make a friend from scratch, you know.

Anyway, the coast was all clear when I got to her locker, so I opened it quickly and taped the invitation to the front of the shelf where there was no way she would miss it. I was sorry I didn't have more to leave, but I knew I'd make up for it the next day, and I was just about to close the metal door and go when my eye caught a glimpse of something oddly familiar. . . .

It was poking out of a plastic bag lying on the bottom of her locker, and it was fluffy and fuzzy and kind of shimmery, and almost exactly the same color as both a blueberry smoothie *and* Claire's new hat and scarf.

I couldn't help it. I reached down and touched it and, yes, peered through the bag some more. There were some knitting needles, plus some pretty green yarn, a few sheets of patterns, and a pack of cinnamon gum. . . .

And I suddenly realized I knew *a lot* about Mia after all. She was Claire's Secret Santa. Not mine at all!

*   *   *

119

I was literally in a daze for the rest of the day. I mean, I totally missed out when Abby passed around her new candy cane lip gloss at lunch, and I *almost* ate my mac and cheese after Colin sneezed all over it. Gross!

In fact, between trying to gauge Mia's reaction to Claire's invitation, which I could see she brought to lunch, and trying to guess who else from homeroom could be such a lame Secret Santa if she wasn't mine, I don't think I even looked at Nick Holiday once!

And it was torture, let me tell you, not to tell Claire what I'd found out. Especially when she asked not once, but at least a dozen times during gym, "So who do you think knows how to knit in our class besides *you*?" along with, "You know, it really worked out well that you had Mia and she had you."

I mean, I couldn't even tell her I didn't think Mia was my Secret Santa anymore. Then she'd have asked me, "Why?" And I'd have had to say, "Uh . . . I don't know. . . ." And she'd have said, "Oh, yes you do! Tell me now or I'll tell Nick you like him!" She thinks she's funny, you know.

All I could tell her was, "Maybe you should get Nick that harmonica, after all." I don't know why, exactly. I just did.

I was actually happy to get home that day — even to my drab, sleigh-on-the-roof-less, deer-on-the-lawn-less house. And I was happy to see my mom looking so happy to see me.

"How was school, Noel, honey?" she asked as I found her in the dining room.

"Interesting," I said.

"Mmm!" She looked up, a little surprised. "That's a new one. Learn a lot?"

"Yeah, kind of," I said. "Hey, what are you doing?"

She had a large cardboard box in front of her on the table and she was just about to open it with a pair of big orange scissors.

She wiggled her eyebrows. "You'll see." Then she slashed and unfolded and lifted out a white plastic candle with a shiny gold plastic base. "Can I tell you I've been looking for these every-where!" she said. "How they ever ended up in the garage under your dad's box of old trophies, I'll never know."

She took out another one and grinned. "Oh, and your dad said he'd get another string of out-door lights for the balsam tree this evening. You're absolutely right about needing to decorate it. It's just getting so big, you know. It's not that simple a project anymore." She paused. "Feel better now?"

I nodded, then I stepped up and gave her a big hug (or the best that I could, considering, you know).

"I love you, Mom," I said. I don't know why, exactly. But I just felt like saying it, you know.

"I love you, too, honey. Ooh! Did you feel that?"

In fact, I did. A big, stiff kick — right in the ribs, too. I mean, *Uh!*

"Whoa." My mom grinned. "I think the baby's trying to say that he or she loves you, too." She pulled out one of the tall-backed chairs and leaned back until she sat down. "I think I need a second," she said. She breathed in deeply and let it out. "But don't worry, hon, these candles will be up before it gets dark tonight, I promise."

She held my hand and squeezed it.

"Why don't I just put them out right now?" I said.

It wasn't any great revelation or anything, as Mrs. Bailey would say, but I swear my mom looked at me as if I had rediscovered the wheel.

"Would you?" she said. "You know what to do?"

(Duh! Put them in front of each window. I think so.)

"That would be great!"

"Cool." I picked up the box and started to carry it out of the room.

"Oh, and they'll need batteries," she told me. "I bought a big pack this morning. You're the best, Noel, honey. Look in the kitchen by the back door."

By the time the candles were fully loaded (not a small job, by the way), my sister Cecee was home from school and buzzing around me like some hyperactive, all black, stripeless bee.

"The candles! Sweet! Are you putting them up? Oh, sweet! Can I help you? Please!"

"I can do it by myself," I assured her.

"Oh, let me help you! Please!"

I'm sure I shook my head. I might have even turned away. "It's a one-person job, Cecee." (I mean, come on, it *is*.) "I'm sorry."

"But that's no fair," she argued. "Please!"

Now, normally — or at least lately — I'd have just said "No." Or maybe yelled it. And she'd have run and told Mom. And Mom would have hollered for me. And I'd have ignored her until I was done. And then I'd have gotten my way and Cecee would have gotten some consolation prize from Mom — a cookie or computer time, or first dibs at the TV. Win-win, if you ask me.

But as I turned and looked at her, all trembly lipped and puppy-dog eyed, I suddenly couldn't help but mutter, "Oh, okay."

Really.

I mean, I'm not sure if I wanted to please her, or spare Mom, or maybe both. I'm not even sure if maybe I *wanted* to do it together. I just know I took out an armful of candles and handed them to her.

"You do the downstairs," I told her. "I'll do up."

And I know that when we all went outside to look at the candles when we were done, Cecee jumped around like a maniac and my mom kept squeezing my hand.

❄CHAPTER ELEVEN❄

Wednesday was a great night. So great that I completely forgot to work on my social studies report at all!

At least, not until Claire called me, but by then it was eight-thirty and, I don't know, it was just so hard to get started.

Clearly I'd be staying up the whole night on Thursday.

But at least I put together a whole... (Um, what's the Christmas equivalent of a cornucopia? Do you know?)... of Secret Santa stuff for Mia (and got to watch *A Charlie Brown Christmas*, which my family had kindly TiVoed for me the night before).

On Thursday, I got to school early and *re*decorated Mia's locker... I had shiny paper chains that Cecee had helped me put together, more glitter-glue-covered snowflakes, and even one of two plastic candles we had left over at home. (For some reason my mom didn't want us to do the attic . . . and I think she let Cecee take the other one to school with her; who knows what for.)

And that wasn't all!

From the center hook, I hung a gift bag, all covered with silver and white angels, which held a ball of sparkly silver and white yarn and directions for making a choker (a really cool one), plus a matching headband that I had made myself. (At first, I'd planned to make both for Mia . . . but *that* was completely insane. Besides, I thought, if *I* was Mia, I'd appreciate a project to do as much as something already made, and I hoped she'd feel the same.)

Then finally, instead of covering all her pictures up with bows and wrapping paper, I framed them with these cute magnetic frames we'd originally bought for our own fridge. (Then we'd found out that magnets don't *stick* to stainless steel . . . so we ended up just using masking tape instead.)

It all looked extremely awesome, if I did say so myself. (And I have to say, I did.) Then I did just one thing more: I took the plastic candle and twisted the flame-shaped bulb about half a turn till it flickered on, and closed the door.

"That looks cool," said a sixth grader as I turned to go.

She pointed to the top vent, through which you could just barely see the candle glow.

"Thanks." I smiled. "I know."

By the time I got to the hall outside Mrs. Bailey's room, most of my friends were at their lockers doing their usual "I love it!"s and "Hurry! Hurry! Check this out!"s, and I dutifully stopped in front of Olivia's to "ooh" and "ahh" over the red and green beaded friendship bracelet she'd just been so thrilled to find.

I cut my eyes to Isabelle, who was hovering nearby. She was really good at friendship bracelets. I winked at her and she smiled. *Hmm,* I thought, *maybe I should be a private eye.*

Then I moved on to my own locker, relieved and a little surprised to notice that for the first time that week I wasn't completely and totally obsessed with what I was going to find.

"Hey, there!" said Claire, walking up, still all bundled in her sister's old coat (which I know she hated), and her new scarf and hat (which, of course, she loved).

"Hey." I smiled back.

"How much did you get done last night?" she asked.

"On my paper?" I said. "Not much."

"Ooh, Noel . . ." She made a rather pained I'm-your-best-friend-and-I-wish-I-could-help-you-but-I-really-don't-see-how-I-can face.

I held up my hand. "I know. I know. But I'll do it tonight. I *know*. Let's just get through today, shall we?"

She laughed. "Okay. Hey." She lowered her voice a notch. "Is Nick here yet, do you know?"

I shook my head. "I haven't seen him. But I just got here. What do you have for him today?"

She swung her backpack over her shoulder and unzipped the front pocket partway. Inside, on top of some tissues, some Mentos, a bright green highlighter, and little foil-wrapped chocolate Santas left over from the day before, was a package wrapped in Claire's snowman-hockey paper, about the size of a hot dog.

"It's the harmonica," she whispered. "Just like you said. And I printed some songs out off the Internet. Lots of Beatles . . . and *The Simpsons* theme song. What do you think?"

"He's gonna love it," I told her. "Let me put my stuff away and I'll help you put it in."

"Cool," she said.

With that, I spun my lock clockwise a few times and dialed my combination again, then yanked the latch and pulled it open . . . and stared in what I think you'd call utter disbelief.

"Whoa!" I said. And I am not kidding: I swung the door back shut to make sure the locker number was really mine.

"What? More socks?" asked Claire, running up from her own locker to peer over my shoulder.

"Not even," I said. "Check it out."

Inside was a big bag of plain M&M's, with a bow tied around it, plus more bows tied on the hooks, each holding two or three awesome little pins just like the kind I collect: a Rudolph, a snowman, a Santa (of course), a peace sign, a Betty Boop, something kind of like a happy face (only it was green and looked really mean), a "Stop Global Warming, Save the Polar Bears," a Halloween one with a witch flying on a broom, a LOVE stamp, a Fall Out Boy, the state of Texas, a winking e-mail face, a "Got Milk?" (had that one already, of course), and get this, four letter pins that spelled NOEL. I know! How cute!

And no, that wasn't all either.

"Look at the arrows!" said Claire.

"Yeah," I said. "I know."

There was one pointing to my pin cup, saying

SECRET SANTA SAYS LOOK! And one pointing to the bottom of my locker saying SECRET SANTA SAYS LOOK AGAIN!

I picked up my pin cup first and noticed right away that it had at least a dozen new ones.

"That Green Day one's cool!" said Claire. "Are these all from today, do you think?"

I bit my lip. "I don't know." I hadn't really been checking my pin cup — just grabbing my books, getting mad, and slamming the door. For all I knew, my Secret Santa could have been leaving me new pins each day, and I hadn't even noticed. What an idiot I was!

"So what's down at the bottom?" she asked.

I bent down and reached in and found a thin, clear plastic case behind my science lab notebook. Inside it was a silver CD with "Secret Santa Mix" written across it in dark red ink.

"That is so cool," said Claire.

"Yeah, I know," was all I could say. *How long has it been there?* I wondered. I wanted to run up to the computer lab and listen to it right that minute.

But Claire was dragging me away. "Come on," she said. "If you still want to help me do Nick's locker, we'd better hurry up."

*　　*　　*

So we did Nick's locker and got to homeroom, though I'll admit all I could think about the whole time was my Secret Santa. So if it wasn't Mia, who *was* it? Was it just a big coincidence that they finally seemed to get a clue . . . or had they heard me in the assembly, too? They must have, right? Don't you figure? I tried to remember who else had been sitting around me . . . but I flat out could not think who.

So I sat down at my desk and scoured the room. . . .

Meanwhile, Mrs. Bailey, in yet *another* sweater — a big Christmas tree, with dangling, gold-beaded garlands and a silver-sequined star at the top — was talking.

"Good morning, class! I hope the open window isn't too much on you all in the back, but when I got in this morning the heat was unbearable." She fanned herself and shook her head as the radiator hissed and clanked behind her back.

I slid my feet out of my shoes and wiggled my red — well, maybe purple — toes merrily around. The room felt good, if you asked me. I mean, I never would have said this, but I did wonder if Mrs. Bailey had thought about just taking off her fifty-pound sweater?

"Let me know if you get too cold back there, all

right?" Mrs. Bailey went on. She nodded especially toward Mia, who was the closest to the window, but when I turned I swear she looked about the happiest I'd ever seen her. She was wearing the headband I'd made, I noticed, and she smiled almost warmly back at Mrs. Bailey as she nodded.

"Very good," said Mrs. Bailey. "Now . . ." She crossed her arms so that they cut her tree in half. "As I'm sure you're aware, it's day four of our Secret Santa — My, just one more day of school!" She clasped her hands eagerly in front of her. "And I hope you've gotten as much out of this project as . . . well, as I hoped." She looked around and surveyed the nods and varying degrees of "Yeah"s and "Uh-huh"s.

"Wonderful," she said. "I mean, it's a silly thing, really, I know. But the consequences can still be big ones — for Santas and for their giftees — which is why . . ." She crossed her arms again. ". . . we'll be spending this period — and tonight, as well, if you have to — writing about what this experience has meant to you."

She paused as responses transitioned quickly to "What?"s, "Really?"s, and "Huh?"s.

"Well, you certainly didn't think this was going to be an exercise without any *writing* component, did you?" Mrs. Bailey raised her thin, dark eyebrows and grinned. "But don't worry, it shouldn't be hard. I want you to feel free to express your emotions. How it felt to have to think about what the other person might like and want. And if you didn't know them well, how it felt to get to know them better. Think about how you felt when you knew they'd received the gift you gave them. And, of course, how it felt to be surprised yourself."

Colin spoke up at the same time he raised his hand.

"Uh, is a paragraph enough?" he asked.

Mrs. Bailey worked her lips into a thin, straight line, framed by wrinkles, like a zipper. "I doubt it," she said simply. "These will be graded, you should know." Then she smiled. "And tomorrow, *if* you want to, you can share your essay with the class. Oh, and that's not all. Tomorrow," she added, "you can all finally reveal whose Secret Santa you were."

"Yes!" cheered a few kids.

"Oh, goody!" snickered Ruby.

I don't think I can wait! I thought to myself.

"Yes, Melanie? What do you want to ask?"

"I won't be here tomorrow," Melanie said, finding a way to remind us *again* of her plans for vacation. "I'm leaving for Costa Rica, remember?"

"Ah, yes," said Mrs. Bailey. She nodded, then apologetically held out her hands. "I suppose you'll just have to wait to find out who your Santa is after vacation then."

I nodded with satisfaction. *You can't have it all,* I thought to myself.

"Okay," said Mrs. Bailey, "let's see those papers and pencils or pens."

We dove after our supplies (or maybe drifted is more like it) and I was just getting to that first step in all my writing — staring at my empty paper — when the classroom door creaked open.

"Ms. Joseph," said Mrs. Bailey, who clearly seemed surprised to see the dark-suited, tight-bunned figure of the principal strolling in. "Good morning. How can we help you?"

"Good morning," said Ms. Joseph, in that I'll-be-the-judge-of-that way she has. She looked around suspiciously. "I say, it's warm in here, isn't it?"

"I *know.*" Mrs. Bailey nodded. "That's why I told maintenance. It seems the colder it gets outside, the hotter it gets in here. Thanks for checking."

Ms. Joseph held up her hands. "Actually, that's not why I'm here."

"Oh," said Mrs. Bailey.

"I'm here," said Ms. Joseph, scanning the room with a squinty-eyed frown, "for Noel Moore."

I think I coughed *and* choked as every eye in the room turned and zeroed in on me.

What did I do? I wondered. (And I know everyone else did, too.) Was it the candle in the locker? Was it some kind of fire code violation? Had that phony little sixth grader gone and told on me? It wasn't a *real* candle, didn't she know? How'd she know my name, anyway? And how could I find out hers?

"Noel?" said Mrs. Bailey, nodding toward me, rather stunned.

I tried to both breathe and sit up straighter. But it seemed that I could only manage one.

"Yes?" squeezed out of my throat in a voice not at *all* my own.

"Ah, Noel," said Ms. Joseph, her face seeming, thankfully, to grow a little softer. "Your grandmother's in the office, dear. She's come to take you to the hospital. Your dad and mom are already there. I guess you're about to have a new sibling."

I could see perfectly well that she was smiling as she said this, and when I looked to her right, Mrs. Bailey was smiling, too. Around me, my friends were clapping and laughing and saying things like "Congratulations!" But all I could think was, *What are you* talking *about? Don't you peo-ple* know*?*

I mean, didn't they know that my mom wasn't supposed to have her baby for another whole *month* still? Didn't they know that if she was in the hospital, something must be terribly *wrong*? Didn't they know that my poor baby sister — or, who knew, brother — might at this very minute be in mortal *danger*? Didn't they *care*?

Please! I was already pleading. *Please let my mom and the baby be okay!* I wouldn't care if I had to take a French test every day. I wouldn't care if my family never went on a vacation again. I wouldn't care if Nick *never* liked me. *Just please let them both be okay,* I begged, *and I'll never, ever, ever, ask for anything again!*

Then I grabbed my bag and my books — at least most of them, as I remember — and ran right by the principal, straight out of the room.

❄ CHAPTER TWELVE ❄

So, my mom had her baby on Thursday afternoon. And it was fine, and so was she.

I mean, it's really, *really* tiny. More like a puppy, if you ask me. But it's got all its parts and it's still pretty cute. (In fact, my mom says it looks a lot like me when I was born.) Oh yeah. And guess what! It's a boy.

We named him Jan after, yes, good old Grandma Janice. I told them a name like that might cause some problems, you know, later on. But like they ever listen to me? And the way they say it, it rhymes with "Ron," not "Stan" — and, I guess, in a way, it does kind of suit him, you know.

He has to stay in the hospital for a few more days, since he's so early and teeny and tiny and all. But we all get to see him during visiting hours, which is kind of creepy (I do *not* like hospitals), but also kind of fun (the nurses are really nice and treat us all like VIPs).

"If we're lucky," my dad told us, "the doctor says he'll be home by Christmas!"

"Aw, shoot," muttered Cecee.

"What?" we all asked her.

"That's too late! Now he can't be Jesus in the Christmas pageant."

"Hey." My dad just shrugged. "You know, Cecee, what can you do?"

My mom didn't even come home from the hospital until just before the pageant on Sunday afternoon, but she gave us careful instructions on Thursday night before we left her.

"First," she said. "I think we've all had a big day today, and I don't think either Noel or Cecee should have to go to school tomorrow."

"Aw!" complained Cecee. "But I have to go. We're having a party. No one will have fun if *I* don't go."

Good old Cecee.

"Well, then, by all means *go,*" my mother told her. She turned to me. "And you?"

"Oh, I think you're *right,* Mom," I told her. "And I'm pretty sure the school can manage without me for one day." I tried not to make *too* obvious the thoughts that were skipping through my head already: No school tomorrow meant no French test and no world history paper to turn in!

"Good," said my mom. "So Paul, be sure to call the school tomorrow to tell them she's staying home. I'm sure they'll understand completely. And maybe she could help you out a little around the house. . . ." She went and did that hairy eyeball thing that always tells you something's up. "We still have that *project* to finish, you know."

"That's right," said my dad, "we do."

"What?" asked Cecee. "What is it?"

"Well, if you must know," my mom said, "we've decided to move you, Cecee, into Noel's room."

"What!" cried Cecee and I at once, together. "What do you mean? That's so not fair!"

"Hang on, hang on," Mom shushed us. She tried to wave her hands, but all the tubes in the left one stopped her.

"Let your mother finish, why don't you?" My father looked at her and smiled.

"Yes, as I was saying . . ." she went on, politely ignoring what I can only imagine was my bitter, how-could-you-Mother? glare. (And I won't even get into Cecee's.) "We've decided to move the baby into Cecee's room, and Noel into the attic."

"The attic?" said Cecee and I at exactly the same time.

I think we both jumped up to hug her at exactly the same time, too.

"Careful," said my mom as we landed on her bed.

"So *I'll* be nearest the baby?" said Cecee. "Can I rock him if he cries?"

"Well, I suppose so," said my mom.

"And I get the attic?" I asked, just to be sure I heard her right. "The whole thing? All to myself?"

My mom laughed a little and nodded. "All to yourself. A real teen palace. Though it still needs a little work." She nodded to my dad, who'd pulled up the hospital room's one ancient, puke-green, vinyl-covered chair. "We've pretty much cleaned it all out," she said, "but I'd hoped to pick out some paint colors and stuff before the baby came . . . and of course we'll want to make Cecee's old room over into something a little more appropriate for a baby boy."

"Oh, I know just what to do!" piped in Cecee.

"Great!" said my mom. "Maybe you guys and Dad can even start decorating this weekend?"

"Can we, Dad?" we pleaded.

He scanned our three pairs of eager eyes and swallowed the idea with one of his funny gulps of dread. "Sounds great," he said. (And yes, that would be called sarcasm.)

"Lovely," said my mom. "Oh, and Noel, don't you have Claire's party tomorrow night?"

I nodded. "Uh-huh."

"Paul, darling, make sure you take her to that . . . and, I don't know, maybe you could take Cecee ice-skating with a friend?"

"Yeah!" she hollered.

"Sounds great," my dad said. (And yes, that was sarcasm again.)

Have I mentioned that the snow started falling that same day that my brother was born? Well, it did. The first snow of the winter. And though it wasn't enough to close school on Friday (as if *I* really cared), or even make it start late, it did cover the ground with a serious white blanket that instantly made everything seem dreamy, new, and clean. It also froze my feet.

Hmm, this could be a problem, I realized, as I shuffled down Claire's slippery front walk toward her brightly lit, be-wreathed-and-bowed, already humming house.

My mom, I knew, wouldn't have let me out without boots on. But my dad wouldn't have noticed if I'd worn a bathing suit, I bet.

At least the inside of Claire's house was dry and cozy, all twinkly and smelling like some great, northern forest full of pine (from candles, of course, since her dad insisted on fake trees, even when they weren't going away). And the wild reception that greeted me made me forget my lack of appropriate footwear for at least a little while.

"Noel! You're here! We missed you! What is it? A boy or a girl?"

I filled them all in on the details, repeating my story at least twenty times (including twice to Claire's mom, who kept having to go tell Claire's brother to turn his music down, upstairs).

"Enough about me, though," I told them. "And yes, you can all come over to see my brother *and* my new room. Now I want to hear about *everything* I missed today at school!"

"Well," began Claire coyly, "we had a French test, as you know. . . ."

"Not me," said Olivia. "I'm taking Spanish. We watched a movie."

"You know I'm not talking about *that*," I said. "What happened in English with the Secret Santas!"

"Oh, *that* . . . " said Claire.

"Yes, *that*," I said. "Who had who?"

"Whom," Claire said.

"Who!"

"Well, you were totally right," she told me. "Tallulah had Ruby, and Ruby totally had Cole."

"And Colin had me." Olivia laughed. "Who would have thought? His gifts were so awesome!"

"*He* gave *you those*?" I pointed in wonder at the Rudolphs with sparkly, jewel noses dangling merrily from her ears.

"Mm-hmm."

"That is so totally cute!"

"I know." Olivia shook her head to make her reindeer dance even more. She laughed. "He's such a goof . . . but I think I'm going to go thank him again!"

Claire and I watched her walk into the kitchen, where the drinks and the tacos and most of the boys were. Then I turned to Claire. "And you?"

"Oh, you'll never, *ever* guess!" she said.

"Mia." I grinned.

She stared at me. "How'd you know?"

"I have my ways. . . ." I fixed her scarf for her at the place where the two crossed ends had fallen to the front. "Hey, is she here?" I wondered.

"Not yet," said Claire. "But she said this morning she would come."

"Good," I said. "Oh, Claire! I have something for you. Hey, can we go upstairs real quick — before Mia comes?"

"Totally!" said Claire. "I have something for you, too!"

We ran up to the room she shared with her sister and she grabbed a small box off of her desk. It was wrapped in the same snowman-hockey paper she'd used for Nick, and as I opened it up eagerly, I couldn't help but laugh.

"Oh my gosh!" I said as the lid came off. "It's the earrings I love!" (You know, those candy cane ones!) "Thanks so much!"

I hugged her and handed her the box (wrapped in Santa-kitten paper, naturally) that I'd brought to the party with me, and hurried to trade in my old, boring peridot earrings for the new ones.

They looked, no doubt about it, even cuter than I'd hoped.

"Ooh!" Claire exclaimed, meanwhile. "Thank you, Noel! I love it so much!"

She held up the gold-and-silver choker I'd spent the day knitting for her and right away began to tie it around her throat. "Thank you! Thank you! How does it look?"

"Awesome." The honest truth.

Then suddenly her mom's voice drifted up from below. "Claire! Where are you? You have more guests arriving, you know!"

"Oops. We better go."

"Just one more thing," I said quickly as we headed for the door. "Remember those Santa socks I gave you . . . do you think, um, I could maybe have them back?"

She grinned as her eyes flashed to my feet. "No problem."

So *this* is why they make socks, I thought, as my feet immediately began to thank me, and I leaned close to Claire as we hurried down the stairs.

"Okay," I said, "now tell me. Who had *me*? I've got to know!"

Claire stopped and crossed one arm in front of her and put her other finger to her cheek.

"Good question," she said.

"Claire!"

She laughed. "Well, I'm not sure it's my place to tell you. . . ." she said. "Did you happen to listen to that CD?"

"Of course," I said. "Fifty times. It's great. I love it. But it's just songs. . . ."

"They didn't *remind* you of anyone?" Claire went on.

"Uh, no," I said. I tried hard to recall each word of each and every song. She was *torturing* me! Truly!

"Like who?"

"Like him." She looked past me, over the railing toward the counter in the kitchen.

I turned. "Billy Butcher? Really?" I said.

"No," she groaned. "Beside him."

I lost my breath for a second and raised my hands to try to catch it.

"No way!" I said, grabbing Claire. It was . . .

Oh, but you've already guessed it, I bet, haven't you? Yep. Bingo! Nick.

I can practically guarantee that I was staring at him like a fool, because of course he looked up and caught me . . . as he *always* seems to do.

I looked down at my damp, canvas-covered feet, and felt Claire nudge . . . no. Push? No. Let's say *shove* me the rest of the way down the stairs.

Then I looked up and there was Nick with half a grin and two full cups of hot chocolate. He offered one to me.

"Uh, thanks," I said.

He kept his semi-smile, but let it roll from right to left. "It's the least a Secret Santa could do," he said. "Surprised. Or did you know?"

"No, I didn't. I swear!" I told him. "I had absolutely no idea. I mean, *obviously*!" I tried to laugh. I wanted to cry. "Or I never would have complained . . . *really*! I mean, I thought . . . well, I thought . . . never mind." Not exactly a story, I realized, that I was *proud* to share with him. So I raised my hand and waved it around as if I could

146

shoo the whole week away. (I wished!) "No. I didn't know you were my Secret Santa. Not at all."

"Well, I'm really sorry," he said. "I was a total jerk for forgetting your combination that first day. Mrs. Bailey had to get Ms. Joseph to say it was okay for the office to give it to me and everything. . . . And then, well, I guess I'm not the best *decorator*. . . ."

"Oh no." I shook my head like a maniac, I'm sure. "No, no, no. Don't be sorry. Please! *I'm* the freak that never even noticed all those pins. Which I love, by the way! And the CD . . ."

"Did you like it?"

"I love it!" I said. And trust me, I really, really did! "And peanut M&M's," I added. "They're not bad at all!"

"I thought you liked them," he said, looking puzzled and kind of surprised. "You sure did eat a lot last summer."

I don't think I said much then. I certainly didn't say, "Oh, that was only because it was a good excuse to talk to you!" No, I don't think so.

"And then there's the socks." He rolled his eyes. "Man, I really got that all wrong. I mean, I knew you never wore them. But here I thought . . ." He shrugged. ". . . that maybe you *needed* them or something." He stretched his neck to look around me at more kids coming in the door. "How are your feet doing out in *that,* by the way?" he asked me.

I took a sip of my cocoa and might have blushed some as I smiled. "Don't tell anyone," I whispered. Then I reached down and pulled up the leg of my cranberry cords.

Nick laughed and hit my shoulder, spilling hot, milky brown liquid down over the whole head of poor, smiling Santas.

"Oops! Sorry!" he said.

"No problem," I told him. (I mean, what would you have said?) I bent and dried them — mostly — with a napkin, then smoothed my pants back down. "I have another pair at home." I smiled, half to make him feel better, and half with relief that the hot chocolate was only warm.

"So . . . how was your Santa?" I asked, almost afraid. "You, um, know that it was Claire?"

"Oh yeah," he answered, nodding. He looked around to find her refilling a big basket of tortilla chips with her mom. Her sister was standing behind her, putting sprinkles on cupcakes. (Her dad, I bet, was somewhere vacuuming, or disinfecting toilet seats.)

"You kind of seemed, I don't know, disappointed in some things. . . ." I said.

148

"Oh no," he assured me. "Not at all. It might have looked like that, I guess, but that's 'cause I was kind of bummed about you."

"You were?"

"Yeah, sure. First I lose your combination. Then I give you stuff you hate — or at least I thought so — when I really wanted to give you good stuff." He looked *right* at me — for a second — then quickly looked away. "But no, Claire's stuff was awesome, and I told her."

"Really," I said, and I think my whole chest sank to my feet. I *knew* he'd end up liking her. I guessed it was just . . . meant to be.

I stared down at my hands as he said, "She said you helped with everything, too."

"She did?" My head popped back up.

"Uh-huh. She said all the Colts stuff, the harmonica, the *peanut* M&M's . . . all your ideas." He was, yeah, I'd have to say, smiling. "How'd you know?"

How did I *know*? I suppose I could have said, "Well, because I spy on you. Because I eavesdrop on all your conversations. Because I think about you constantly. Because you're my crush and, well, that's just what you do. Come to think of it, how'd you know so much about what I liked, too . . . ?"

I could have. But I didn't.

What I said was, "I dunno." Then I guess I sighed and said, "I just wish I'd known as much about what my own person wanted."

"What do you mean?" asked Nick. "Didn't you have Mia?"

"Yeah," I said. "Exactly." I think I made a face and nodded.

"But in class today she said you were basically awesome."

I looked at him *again*. "She did?"

"Yeah." He looked back at me and smiled this sweet, amazing smile. "She said the only thing she wished is that you'd known she couldn't eat nuts. Peanuts especially. She's allergic. Oh, and that she doesn't have pierced ears." He shrugged.

I cringed. "Oh, that wasn't good." I felt like such a stupid jerk.

"Nah." Nick shook his head. "She said it was all good in the end . . . the knitting meant a lot. Go ask her yourself." He nodded back toward Claire's front door, through which Mia'd just come in.

Claire's dad was taking her coat (with the hand not clutching the DustBuster), and she was looking. She looked around at everyone talking and eating, not seeming to know what to do. She was wearing a cute, fuzzy sweater and the headband I'd made for her, too.

"I guess..." I said to Nick, "...I should go over and say hi." I mean, she looked so alone there, and like she could turn at any second and go. It was a look, I know, I'd have thought at one time was just rude. Stuck-up. Whatever. Suit yourself. Who cares. Just go.

It wasn't that at all, though, was it? It was just plain shy.

The only problem with leaving Nick, though, was that my Santa- (and chocolate-) covered feet didn't seem to want to move.

"I'll go with you," Nick said. "Come on."

There was an instant feeling in my stomach that was much more than a flutter. It was more like some big bird — a goose or something — trying to take off from a lake.

We walked over . . . together.

"Hi, Mia," I said. "I'm, uh, glad that you could come."

"Thanks." She smiled, kind of relieved and kind of self-conscious, I think. "Um . . . did your mom have her baby?"

"Yep." I nodded. I couldn't help but smile, I know. "It's a boy. He can't come home yet. He's too little. But he's really cute and we named him Jan."

"No way," said Mia. "My brother's named Jan, too."

She looked completely stunned, and I think I must have, too.

"You're kidding, right?" said Nick. "Your parents *both* picked a name like that?"

We both looked at him and frowned.

"Uh, sorry," he said.

"Watch it," I teased him. (I mean, of course, it was *okay*.)

"That's so funny," I said to Mia. "Is he older or younger . . . ?"

"He's two."

"Ooh," I said. "How is that?"

"It's okay. He's pretty cute. He likes it here a lot. You know, lots more space to run around."

"How about you?" I asked — though I guess I kind of knew the answer.

"It's . . . okay." Mia shrugged. "I liked New York. My friends and I used to knit at this little shop sometimes after school. I miss it. I miss them. . . ." She shrugged again. "You know."

"Yeah, we don't really have any place like that," I said. "But" — a thought occurred to me — "you could come over to my house to knit."

"Yeah?" She looked . . . I don't know, is "flabbergasted" really a word?

"Sure," I said. "Anytime. Why don't you call me when you get back from break?"

"Oh, we're not going away," she said. "My mom says we have too much to do."

"Really?" I said. "I'm staying home, too!"

"That makes three of us," Nick said.

I turned. Can you believe I'd actually forgotten he was there?!

"Well . . ." I said, suddenly feeling like I'd won some kind of middle-school, winter-break lottery or something. (Maybe misery *does* love company, after all . . . you know?) "Maybe we should all do something together? I mean, don't you think?"

"Totally!"

So what am I doing right now? Getting ready to knit a hat for my new baby brother, pattern courtesy of Mia. (Honestly, his head's so small, I bet I'm done in, like, an hour.)

And where am I doing it? In my brand-new room (aka the still-unpainted attic).

And where am I going *tonight*? Ice-skating with Nick and Mia! (And, I have a feeling, Cecee will go, too.)

Boy, was I wrong about Mia. She is not stuck-up at all. Can you believe she thought *we* didn't want to be friends with *her*? Where in the world did she ever get that idea, I'd like to know.

Plus, according to Mia, I might have been wrong about Nick, too. She swears she thinks he likes me — and not just in that "friend" way either, you know. She says she's thought so since October — the way he looks at me all the time. I honestly don't know what she's talking about . . . but maybe we'll find out a little more tonight!

Tomorrow, I'll probably make a gingerbread house with Cecee to surprise Mom with when she and Dad bring Jan home.

Then it's Christmas! Then New Year's! (Guess who's invited to Nick's house, by the way!) Then . . . Valentine's Day!

I can't even wait, I mean, can you?

Sure, sometime this week I'll have to write my history report. (And I've finally decided what to do it on: this awesome festival called Raksha Bandhan, where sisters and brothers celebrate their love for each other!) Then I guess I have to write that essay for English, too. I don't know . . . maybe I should just give Mrs. Bailey this. What do you think?

Whatever. The bottom line is this: I *do* love the holidays as much as the next girl. . . .

I don't know . . . who knows? Maybe even a little more!